Divine Detours

Part 2

The Thornton Family Saga

#1 International Bestselling Author
Angela R. Edwards

Divine Detours – Part 2
The Thornton Family Saga

Angela R. Edwards

Pearly Gates Publishing LLC
INSPIRING CHRISTIAN AUTHORS TO BE AUTHORS

Pearly Gates Publishing, LLC, Harlem, GA (USA)

Divine Detours – Part 2:
The Thornton Family Saga

Scripture references are used with permission via Zondervan at Biblegateway.com.

ISBN 13: 978-1-948853-87-3
Library of Congress Control Number: 2025937688

For information and bulk ordering, contact:
Pearly Gates Publishing, LLC
Angela Edwards, CEO
P.O. Box 639
Harlem, GA 30814
pearlygatespublishing@gmail.com

Dedication

To the cherished readers of Divine Detours:

May you find strength in faith as you navigate life's unexpected paths. Remember, God's guidance shines brightest in moments of uncertainty. Embrace each detour as a divine opportunity to grow closer to Him. Your journey is uniquely yours and filled with insurmountable blessings.

Introduction: The Faith Walk of His Beloved

In life, some threads are woven tighter than others, crafting a narrative of love, faith, and resilience that inspires everyone who witnesses it. Such is the tale of Chloe and Cyrus, a couple whose journey through life's joys and sorrows serves as a testament to the enduring power of faith and the transformative nature of love.

Meet Chloe—a former bright-eyed elementary school teacher with a heart full of compassion and love for her family, students, and God's children.

Meet Cyrus—an earnest young man with an unwavering dedication to his faith and family.

From the moment their paths crossed, it was evident that their connection was something special. Their shared love for God formed the foundation of a relationship that would weather storms and celebrate joys in equal measure. As they began building a life together, Chloe and Cyrus made a solemn vow to keep their faith at the forefront of their relationship—a decision that would become their anchor in life's turbulent seas.

The early years of their marriage were filled with the sweet anticipation of new beginnings. They welcomed their first child, Cullen, with hearts overflowing with gratitude. The sleepless nights and endless diaper changes were met with laughter and prayer, each moment a gentle reminder of the precious gift they had been entrusted with. As their family grew with the additions of Carmel and Chelsea, so did their love for one another and their faith.

BUT life, as it often does, had trials and tribulations in store for the young family. One test came in the form of questioning the paternity of their youngest child. Yet another was a devastating fire that reduced their home to ashes. Standing amid the smoldering ruins of their collective dreams, Chloe and Cyrus clung to each other and their faith. In the face of insurmountable loss, they found strength in the words of Romans 8:28:

"And we know that in all things, God works for the good of those who love Him, who have been called according to His purpose."

That trial, while heart-wrenching, strengthened their bond and deepened their devotion. As they rebuilt their lives, creating a testament to the resilience that stems from a foundation rooted in God's love, their children watched and learned, absorbing the powerful lesson that one can rise from the ashes of adversity with faith and perseverance.

The years that followed brought a mix of joys and challenges. Chloe and Cyrus celebrated their children's milestones: first steps, first words, school graduations—each a reminder of God's blessings. They also faced moments of doubt and fear, particularly when Cullen began questioning his faith during his teenage years. That period tested their patience and beliefs, but it also taught them the value of allowing space for growth and personal discovery in matters of faith. Through open discussions, unwavering love, and constant prayer, they guided Cullen on his spiritual journey. Watching their eldest child emerge from that period of questioning with a stronger, more personal relationship with God was a profound reminder of God's faithfulness and the importance of trusting in His plan.

Perhaps the greatest test of their faith came with the sudden loss of Cyrus' mother, Mrs. Victoria Thornton. Her passing left a void in their lives that seemed impossible to fill. Grief threatened to overwhelm them, testing the very foundations of their faith. Yet, even during that dark time, Chloe and Cyrus turned to each other and God for solace.

In their sorrow, they discovered surprising blessings. The community came together, offering support and love in countless ways. Their children, observing their parents' steadfast faith even amidst loss, gained a deeper understanding of the strength found in a life devoted to God.

Chloe and Cyrus' love for each other and God deepened through every trial and triumph. They became pillars of their community, transforming their home into a haven of love and understanding for everyone who entered. Their children matured into adults, each carrying the lessons of faith, resilience, and love they learned from their parents.

Cullen, a once-questioning teenager, became a pastor. His journey through doubt and discovery allowed him to connect with and guide others in their spiritual struggles. Carmel's passionate spirit led her to a career in social work, where she daily practiced the lessons of love and service she learned in her youth. Chelsea, the youngest of the trio, discovered her calling in art. Her creations were vibrant expressions of the beauty and wonder of God's creation.

As Chloe and Cyrus entered their golden years, they reflected on their journey with hearts full of gratitude. Though challenging, the trials they had faced served to refine their faith and strengthen their love. They recognized God's hand in every chapter of their story, from the joyous highs to the difficult lows.

As we delve deeper into Chloe and Cyrus' love story, we are invited to reflect on our own journeys of faith and love. Their tale reminds us that a life built on the bedrock of faith can endure any storm, that love strengthened by shared beliefs can overcome any obstacle, and that family, when nurtured with patience, understanding, and unwavering devotion, can be our greatest source of strength and joy.

In the following chapters, you will witness the unfolding of a love story that spans decades, weathering trials and celebrating triumphs. You will see how Chloe and Cyrus' faith in God and each other carries them through life's challenges, shaping them into beacons of hope and inspiration for all who know them. Their story is more than just a recounting of events; it is an invitation to examine your life, consider the role of faith in your relationships, and reflect on love's power to transform and uplift.

As we journey with Chloe, Cyrus, and their family through the chapters of their lives, may we find inspiration to deepen our faith, love wholeheartedly, and face life's challenges with courage and grace. Ultimately, it's not the absence of trials that defines a life well-lived, but the presence of faith, the persistence of hope, and the endurance of love. May their story serve as a testament to truth and God's love for His children, acting as a beacon of light that guides us toward a life rich in meaning, overflowing with love, and anchored in unshakeable faith.

Table of Contents

Chapter One: Lessons in Love and Life

The early morning sun streamed through the kitchen window, casting a warm glow on Chloe as she made breakfast for her family. The aroma of freshly brewed coffee blended with the scent of French toast, creating a cozy atmosphere in the Thornton household. Cyrus walked into the kitchen, his tie slightly askew, and kissed Chloe's cheek before tousling five-year-old Cullen's curly hair and playfully tickling three-year-old Carmel's chin.

"Good morning, my loves," Cyrus said, his voice warm with affection. "Who's ready for another day of adventure?"

Chloe smiled, her heart full as she watched her husband interact with their children. "Adventure indeed," she replied, handing Cyrus his travel mug of coffee. "We've got fractions for Cullen and color mixing for Carmel on the agenda today." Chloe couldn't help but feel a mix of excitement and trepidation about the day ahead. Homeschooling their children had been a decision she and Cyrus made together, grounded in their desire to provide a faith-based education and nurture their children's individual gifts. Yet, some days, the challenge of balancing it all felt overwhelming.

Sensing his wife's exhaustion, Cyrus whispered to her, "You've got this." He gently squeezed her hand, his eyes conveying the depth of his love and support. "Remember the words of Proverbs 22:6: *'Start children off on the way they should go, and when they are old, they will not turn from it.'*"

Chloe nodded, drawing strength from his words and the scripture. "Thank you," she said softly. "Have a blessed day at work. We'll be praying for your big presentation!" As Cyrus left for his job at the marketing firm, Chloe turned her attention to the day's lessons. She had learned early on that structure was key to successful homeschooling, but flexibility was equally important. Today, she chose to begin with a nature walk, blending scientific observation with physical activity. "Alright, explorers," she announced cheerfully, "let's gear up for our morning adventure!"

Cullen and Carmel eagerly put on their explorer hats, adorned with leaves, vibrant flowers, and other natural elements—a creative touch introduced by Chloe to make outdoor learning more engaging. As they ventured into the backyard, Chloe marveled at how their spacious property had transformed into an extension of their classroom.

"Mom, look!" Cullen exclaimed, pointing to a vividly bright purple caterpillar inching along a leaf. "Can we learn about butterflies today?"

Chloe smiled, recognizing a teachable moment. "Absolutely! Let's observe it carefully, and then we can research its lifecycle when we go back inside."

As the morning progressed, Chloe guided her children through various subjects, weaving biblical principles with academic concepts. She assisted Cullen with his fractions using apple slices, turning mathematics into a delicious lesson. For Carmel, color mixing became a joyful exploration of God's creativity, with each new shade prompting squeals of delight, especially when she created bubblegum pink.

By lunchtime, Chloe experienced a sense of accomplishment and a wave of fatigue. While the children munched on their sandwiches, she paused to close her eyes and offered a silent prayer of gratitude, asking for strength as well.

'Lord, thank You for the opportunity to educate our children at home. Please grant me patience and wisdom as we go through our day.'

The afternoon presented its own set of challenges. Cullen struggled with a math assignment, and his frustration grew with each attempt. Chloe knelt beside him, speaking gently but firmly. "Remember, sweetheart: It's okay to find things difficult sometimes. That's how we grow. Take a deep breath and try again."

Meanwhile, Carmel had decided that nap time was optional. Her energy level appeared boundless as she bounced from one activity to another. Chloe continually redirected her, all while trying to keep Cullen focused on his schoolwork.

As the clock ticked closer to Cyrus' return, Chloe felt both relief and guilt. She loved homeschooling, but some days left her feeling drained and unsure of her abilities. She yearned for her husband's steady presence and reassuring words.

When Cyrus walked through the door, his face lit up at the sight of his family. Despite the long day in the office, he immediately engaged with the children, listening intently to their excited recounts of the day's lessons before directing his attention to Chloe. "And how was your day, love?" he asked, noticing the slight slump in her shoulders.

Chloe sighed, leaning in his embrace. "It was... full," she replied honestly. "Sometimes, I wonder if I'm doing enough. Am I truly giving them everything they need?"

Cyrus gently cupped her face, his eyes brimming with love and admiration. "Chloe, you are incredible. Our children are thriving because of your dedication and love. Remember: We're in this together. I love you." His words enveloped her, soothing her spirit and reaffirming their partnership in raising their family. Together, they prepared dinner as the kitchen echoed with laughter and stories from their day.

After settling the children into bed for the night, Chloe and Cyrus prayed together, expressing gratitude for their blessings and seeking guidance for the days ahead. Later, as they sat on the porch swing, cherishing a rare moment of quiet,

Chloe turned to Cyrus, her eyes revealing a mix of excitement and apprehension. "Cyrus, I... I think I might be pregnant," she whispered.

The words hung in the air between them, filled with possibility and a touch of uncertainty. Cyrus' eyes widened, a smile slowly spreading across his face. "Really? Oh, Chloe, that's wonderful news!" He pulled her close, his excitement palpable.

Chloe laughed softly, her tears of joy mingling with lingering concerns. "It is wonderful, but I'm also a bit scared. How will we manage with another little one? Homeschooling two is already so demanding..." she said, her voice trailing off, almost as if she were talking to herself.

Cyrus listened attentively, his thumb tracing soothing circles on her hand. "I understand your concerns, love. But remember, we've faced challenges before and always come through stronger because of them. This baby—if you are pregnant—is a blessing from God. We'll figure it out together, just like we always have."

His words were filled with faith and love, calming the racing thoughts in Chloe's mind. She rested her head on his shoulder, feeling a wave of peace wash over her. "You're right," she said softly. "God has always provided for us, even when the path felt uncertain. This is just another delightful detour in our journey."

As they sat together, wrapped in each other's arms and the evening's calm, Chloe reflected on the life they had built together. Balancing homeschooling, Cyrus' career, and family life hadn't always been easy, but their lives were rich with love, faith, and purpose. The potential of a new life growing within her filled Chloe with a renewed sense of wonder at God's plan for their family. She placed a hand on her belly, saying a silent prayer of gratitude and hope for the future.

"What are you thinking?" Cyrus asked, noticing her contemplative expression.

Chloe smiled, her eyes shining with love and determination. "I'm thinking about how blessed we are and how excited I am for this new chapter in our lives. Whatever challenges come our way, I know we can face them together, with God's grace guiding us."

Cyrus nodded and pulled her closer. "Together," he agreed, his voice filled with love and conviction. "Always together."

The stars twinkled overhead as the couple sat in comfortable silence. Their hearts were filled with love for each other, their children, and the potential new life that might be joining their family. They knew the road ahead might have its bumps and turns, but with faith as their compass and love as their strength, they were ready to embrace whatever divine detours lay ahead... or were they?

As they headed inside to prepare for bed, Chloe and Cyrus looked toward the future with hope and excitement, eager to write the next captivating chapter in their ongoing love story.

Chapter Two: Love's Labor

The computer screen's glow illuminated Cyrus' face as he pored over spreadsheets and client proposals late into the night. The house was quiet except for the gentle hum of the air conditioner and the occasional creak of the old farmhouse settling. He rubbed his eyes as fatigue set in, but his mind was far from sleep. His thoughts kept drifting to Chloe, asleep upstairs, her body cradling their unborn child.

From the onset, her pregnancy had been far more complicated than the previous two. The morning sickness seemed relentless, and the tiredness was overwhelming. Cyrus' heart ached every time he saw the dark circles under his wife's eyes or noticed her wincing from the pain in her sides that plagued her. He couldn't shake the memories of her last two pregnancies, the sudden complications that had arisen, and the fear that had gripped them both—only to conclude with the births of two perfect babies.

Cyrus closed his laptop and headed upstairs, his footsteps careful and soft on the old wooden stairs. He paused at the children's rooms, peeking in to see Cullen and Carmel peacefully asleep, their little chests rising and falling rhythmically. A wave of love washed over him, quickly followed by a pang of guilt. He had been so busy with work lately, trying to secure a massive account for the company, but at what cost?

As Cyrus entered the master bedroom, his eyes landed on Chloe's sleeping form. Even in the dim light, he could see the tension in her face and how her hand rested protectively over her growing belly. He gently sat on the edge of the bed, careful not to wake her, and brushed a stray, curly braid from her forehead. "Oh, Chloe," he whispered, his voice barely audible. "What am I doing?" At that moment, as he watched his wife sleep, Cyrus felt a shift within himself. The ambition that had driven him for so long suddenly seemed hollow compared to his family's needs. He thought about the long hours at the office, the missed dinners, and the bedtime stories he hadn't read. Now, with another baby on the way and Chloe struggling, he knew something had to change.

The next morning, Cyrus broached the subject over breakfast. "I've been thinking," he began, observing Chloe sip on ginger tea that had become a remedy for her ongoing nausea. "What if I worked from home more?"

Chloe's eyes widened in surprise as her arm paused halfway to her mouth, teacup in hand. "But what about the big account you've been working on?"

Cyrus reached across the table, taking her hand in his. "That doesn't matter to me at all if you and my family aren't okay. I've been so focused on the business that I've neglected what's truly important."

Tears welled up in Chloe's eyes. "Oh, Cyrus, you haven't been neglecting us. You work so hard for this family."

"But I can work hard and be present at the same time," Cyrus insisted. "I can handle most of my work from home, only going into the office for important meetings. And..." He hesitated, aware that his next words might face resistance. "I think we should consider hiring a nanny to assist with the kids and the homeschooling."

Chloe's brow furrowed. "A... nanny? But I love teaching our children! It's such an essential part of our family life."

Cyrus squeezed her hand gently. "I know, love. And you're the most amazing teacher I've known. But with this pregnancy being so tough and the new baby coming, you need to rest. We can find someone who shares our values—someone to assist you, not replace you." He could see the conflict in Chloe's eyes. The desire to maintain their current lifestyle warred with the undeniable need for help.

After a long, reflective silence, Chloe finally said, "Let's pray about it. Let's seek God's guidance."

Over the next few weeks, Cyrus immersed himself in reorganizing his work life. He had open discussions with his staff, explaining his need for a better work-life balance. To his surprise, they were supportive, recognizing the value of a boss equally dedicated to work and home.

At home, Cyrus took on many of the tasks that had previously fallen to Chloe. He learned the intricacies of their homeschooling curriculum, marveling at the patience and creativity Chloe had always infused into their children's education. He handled meal preparations, filling the kitchen with the aroma of home-cooked dinners and the sound of his off-key singing as he worked.

One evening, as Cyrus helped Cullen with a particularly tricky math problem while simultaneously keeping an eye on Carmel and her art project, he noticed Chloe watching them from the doorway. Her eyes sparkled with love and a hint of amusement. "What?" he asked, a smudge of orange paint on his cheek from when Carmel excitedly showed him her still-wet masterpiece.

Chloe shook her head, smiling. "Nothing. It's just... you're incredible, you know that? The kids are flourishing with you as their teacher. And I..." She placed a hand on her swollen belly. "I feel so supported and loved."

Cyrus stood and crossed the room to embrace his wife. "That's all I want," he murmured into her hair. "For you to feel loved and supported. For our family to be strong and happy."

As the weeks passed, their home settled into a new rhythm. Cyrus found a balance between his work responsibilities and his role as a more present husband and father. He cherished the moments he might have missed before: Cullen's triumphant grin when he finally grasped a difficult concept, Carmel's giggles as she chased butterflies in the garden, and the quiet evenings spent with Chloe, her feet in his lap as they talked about their days.

The decision not to hire a nanny was mutual, reached after much prayer and discussion. Instead, they leaned on their church community, accepting offers of help from friends who brought meals or took the children for playdates to give Chloe a chance to rest.

One lazy Sunday afternoon, while the family relaxed in the living room, Cyrus looked around at his loved ones. Cullen sprawled on the floor, engrossed in a book about dinosaurs. Carmel curled up next to Chloe on the couch, her little hand resting on her mother's belly as she felt for the baby's kicks. With her eyes closed and a serene smile on her face, Chloe looked more relaxed than she had in months. Cyrus's heart swelled with love and gratitude. He realized this was success— not the massive corner office or the impressive title, but this moment of peace and togetherness.

But even as warmth filled his chest, a small seed of unease took root in the back of his mind. He couldn't shake the feeling that his period of tranquility was somehow fragile, that challenges loomed ahead that would test the strength of his love and faith.

As if sensing his sudden tension, Chloe's eyes popped open, meeting his gaze. "Is everything okay, sweetheart?" she asked softly.

Cyrus forced a smile, pushing aside the nagging worry. "Everything's perfect," he replied. As he moved toward the couch, he paused to ruffle Cullen's hair before sitting next to his wife and wrapping his arm around her and their daughter. Yet, even as he basked in the warmth of his family's love, Cyrus couldn't completely silence the foreboding whisper in his heart. He silently prayed, asking God for strength and guidance for whatever lay ahead. For now, though, he would cherish the moment, holding tightly to the precious gift of his family and the love that connected them.

As the afternoon light faded, casting long shadows across the living room, Cyrus couldn't help but wonder what challenges awaited them on the horizon. But as he looked at Chloe, her face aglow with contentment, he knew that whatever came their way, they would face it together. Their love was always a beacon, guiding them through every storm.

Chapter Three: Unspoken Whispers

Candlelight flickered across the table, casting dancing shadows on the faces of Chloe and Cyrus as they sat in the cozy corner of La Petite Maison, the French bistro that had become their favorite dating spot over the years. The familiar aroma of exotic herbs and freshly baked bread enveloped them, evoking memories of simpler times before the whirlwind of marriage and parenthood swept them up.

Cyrus reached across the table, intertwining his fingers with Chloe's. "Do you remember our first date here?" he asked, his deep brown eyes twinkling with nostalgia.

Chloe's lips curved into a smile, but Cyrus couldn't help but notice that it didn't quite reach her eyes. "How could I forget? You were so nervous that you knocked over the breadbasket while trying to impress me with your French."

They shared a laugh, the sound mingling with the soft jazz playing in the background. However, as Cyrus studied his wife's face, he sensed an undercurrent of tension beneath her cheerful exterior. It had lingered for weeks now... a subtle change in her demeanor that he couldn't quite pinpoint.

"Are you feeling alright, love?" Cyrus asked gently, his thumb tracing soothing circles on the back of her hand. "The morning sickness isn't too bad today, I hope. Would you like to leave now?" he asked with genuine concern.

Chloe's free hand instinctively moved to her growing midsection—a gesture that had become increasingly frequent. "I'm fine," she assured him, perhaps a little too quickly. "I'm just a bit tired, that's all."

Cyrus nodded, not entirely convinced but reluctant to push the issue. He had noticed Chloe's hesitance to discuss the pregnancy beyond the most basic details, a stark contrast to her excitement during her previous two pregnancies. However, he reminded himself that every pregnancy was unique, and Chloe had always been someone who processed her emotions in her own time and in her own way.

When their meals arrived—Coq au Vin for Cyrus and Vegetable Risotto for Chloe—they engaged in easier conversation, reminiscing about their courtship and the early days of their marriage. Cyrus entertained Chloe with stories of his awkward attempts to win her heart, and she responded with anecdotes of her own shy hesitations. Even after all those years, Chloe's love had the power to make Cyrus feel like the luckiest man alive. "Chloe, you are the most mesmerizing woman I've ever known. Inside and out." A shadow briefly crossed Chloe's face, so fleeting that he almost missed it.

Before he could question it, Chloe plastered on a bright smile. "Flatterer," she teased, though her voice lacked its usual playful tone.

As the evening progressed, Cyrus became acutely aware of every subtle shift in Chloe's expression, every occasion when her smile wavered, and each time her eyes became distant. He yearned to ask what was bothering her, to reassure her that whatever it was, they could tackle it together. Yet, he held back, recalling his father's advice: "Sometimes, the most loving thing you can do is give your wife space to come to you in her own time."

After dinner, they took a leisurely stroll through the park where they had shared their first kiss long ago. The night air was crisp, carrying the fragrance of blooming jasmine. Cyrus draped his jacket over Chloe's shoulders, drawing her close as they walked. "Do you remember that night?" he asked softly, nodding toward the ornate fountain where they now stood. "I was so nervous. I just knew my heart would leap right out of my chest."

Chloe nestled against him, resting her head on his shoulder. "I remember," she murmured. "I had never felt so cherished, so... seen. You made me feel like the most precious thing in the world."

Cyrus turned to face her, gently cupping her face in his hands. "You are the most precious thing in my world, Chloe.

You and our children mean everything to me. Nothing matters more than your happiness and well-being."

Tears welled in Chloe's eyes, and for a moment, Cyrus thought she might finally share what was troubling her soul. Instead, she pressed her lips to his in a tender kiss, pouring all the words she couldn't express at that moment into that single gesture.

As they made their way home, hand in hand, Cyrus' mind raced with possibilities.

Was Chloe worried about the pregnancy?

Was she having second thoughts about having another child?

Or was it something else entirely, something he couldn't even begin to fathom?

The following weeks brought a series of similar outings: picnics in the countryside, a concert in the park, and even a weekend getaway to a charming bed and breakfast. Each excursion was filled with moments of genuine joy and connection, but there was always an unspoken tension that seemed to be growing between them.

On a lazy Sunday afternoon, as they lay together in a hammock in their backyard while Cullen and Carmel played nearby, Cyrus decided to broach the subject once again. "Chloe," he began, his voice soft yet earnest, "you know you can tell me anything, right? Whatever's on your mind, whatever's troubling you, I'm here. Always."

Chloe remained silent for a long moment, her fingers absentmindedly tracing patterns on Cyrus' chest. When she finally spoke, her voice was barely above a whisper. "I know. And I love you for that. It's just... I'm not ready to talk about it. Not yet."

Cyrus' heart tightened at the evident pain in her voice, but he compelled himself to honor her wishes. "Okay," he said with finality, accepting defeat as he kissed the top of her head. "Whenever you're ready, I'll be here to listen."

As more time went by, Cyrus dedicated himself to making Chloe feel loved and supported in every way he could. He left little notes of encouragement around the house, surprised her with her favorite treats, and assumed even more of the household and homeschooling duties.

One evening, as Cyrus tucked Carmel into bed, the little girl looked up at him with wide, innocent eyes. "Daddy," she said, her voice serious, "is Mommy sad?"

His heart skipped a beat. "What makes you ask that, sweetie?"

Carmel shrugged, clutching her stuffed purple rabbit closely. "She seems sad sometimes. And she doesn't sing as much anymore when she teaches us."

Swallowing the lump in his throat, Cyrus brushed Carmel's hair from her forehead. "Mommy's just a little tired right now because of the baby growing in her tummy. But we can help her feel better by giving her lots of hugs. Can you do that?"

Carmel nodded solemnly, and Cyrus felt a wave of love for his perceptive little girl. As he left her room, he found Chloe standing in the hallway just a few feet from Carmel's bedroom door, tears streaming down her face. "Oh, Chloe," he breathed, pulling her into his arms. She clung to him desperately, her body shaking with silent sobs.

"I'm sorry," she whispered against his chest. "I'm so sorry. I want to tell you. I do. I'm just... I'm so scared."

Cyrus held her tighter, his own eyes stinging with unshed tears. "Whatever it is, we'll face it together. You and me, just like always."

Chloe pulled back slightly, meeting his gaze with red-rimmed eyes. "Promise me," she said, her voice trembling. "Promise me you'll still love me, no matter what."

"I promise," Cyrus replied without a moment's hesitation. Meanwhile, his heart was breaking at the fear reflected in her eyes. "Nothing in this world could ever make me stop loving you, Chloe. Nothing."

As they stood in the dimly lit hallway, holding each other close, Cyrus sensed a shift in the air between them. Whatever secret Chloe was harboring, whatever storm was brewing on their horizon, he knew it was significant and would be life-changing. Still, their love had been tested before and only grew stronger. This time would be no different. Yet, as he led Chloe to their bedroom, his arm protectively around her waist, he couldn't shake the feeling that their lives were about to change in ways he couldn't even begin to imagine. He sent up a silent prayer, asking God for strength, wisdom, and, above all else, the ability to love Chloe through whatever lay ahead.

As they settled into bed, Chloe curled into Cyrus' side, her head resting on his chest. "I love you," she murmured, her voice heavy with emotion. "More than you could ever know."

Cyrus tightened his arms around her, pressing a kiss to her forehead. "I love you, too," he whispered. "Always and forever."

In the stillness of their room, with moonlight streaming through the window, Cyrus held his wife close, his mind racing with unspoken questions. He vowed to himself that whatever challenge they were about to face, they would confront it together. Their love was the beacon that would guide them through the storm.

As sleep finally claimed them both, Cyrus' last conscious thought was a blend of love, concern, and unwavering determination. No matter what lay ahead, he would stand by Chloe's side. Their love was a testament to the enduring power of faith, commitment, and the unbreakable bond of true partnership.

Chapter Four: Love's Gentle Strength

The glow of the bedside lamp cast a warm halo around Chloe as she reclined against a mountain of pillows, her swollen belly a prominent curve beneath the blankets. Cyrus sat on the edge of the bed, his hand gently resting on hers, his eyes filled with love and concern.

"How are you feeling today, love?" he asked, his voice soft and tender.

Chloe managed a small smile, though the strain of weeks spent in bed was clear in the shadows beneath her eyes. "I'm okay," she replied, her free hand absentmindedly rubbing her belly. "I'm just... restless. I miss being able to do things and be with the children."

"I know, sweetheart. But remember what Dr. Anderson said: This bed rest is essential for you and the baby. We're in the final stretch now." As he spoke, a muffled crash echoed from downstairs, followed by Cullen calling out, "Dad, Carmel spilled her juice!" Cyrus closed his eyes for a moment, taking a deep breath. His smile was back in place when he opened his eyes, although Chloe didn't miss the flicker of exhaustion that passed over his face. "Duty calls," he said lightly, giving her hand a squeeze before standing. "I'll be right back. Do you need anything while I'm downstairs?"

Chloe shook her head, signaling no. Her heart ached as she watched Cyrus leave the room. She knew firsthand how difficult it was to work, manage the children, and maintain the household all at once, yet he never complained. He never revealed just how tired he must truly be.

Downstairs, Cyrus found Carmel standing in a puddle of orange juice, her lower lip trembling in fear. "I'm sorry, Daddy," she whimpered. "I didn't mean to do it."

"It's okay, sweetie," Cyrus reassured, lifting her and placing her on a dry section of the floor. "Accidents happen. Let's all clean it up together, alright?" As he and the children mopped up the spill, Cyrus' mind raced with the tasks ahead. He needed to prepare lunch, assist Cullen with his math lesson, ensure Carmel took her nap, and somehow fit in a conference call with his biggest client, who was becoming increasingly impatient with his divided attention.

Once the kitchen was clean and the children were settled with their lunch, Cyrus retreated to his home office. He had just barely sat in his maroon leather office chair when his phone buzzed with a text message from his second-in-command, Fred:

"Cyrus, we need to talk. Boyce & Co. is threatening to pull out of the deal. We need all hands on deck for this one."

Cyrus' stomach dropped to his feet. Boyce & Co. was their biggest client—the one that had kept the business afloat during lean times. Losing them now, with a new baby on the way and mounting medical bills, was unthinkable. He glanced at his watch, remembering he had promised to bring Chloe her lunch soon.

With a heavy sigh, he dialed Fred's number. "Talk to me," he said as soon as Fred answered. "How serious is it?"

As Fred outlined the situation, Cyrus felt the world's weight on his shoulders grow heavier. They needed him in the office immediately to smooth things over with the client personally. But how could he leave Chloe and the children?

"I'll... I'll figure something out," Cyrus said at last. "Give me a day to rearrange things here. We can't afford to lose that account, Fred." After ending the call, he leaned back in his chair, running both hands over his face in frustration. He hadn't shared the struggles at the office with Chloe because he didn't want to add to her stress during this delicate time. But now, with everything hanging in the balance, he wondered if he had made the right decision.

Setting his worries aside, Cyrus arranged a tray with Chloe's lunch: a light Caesar salad and fresh fruit, just as the doctor had advised. He put on a smile as he climbed the stairs, determined not to let his concerns show. "Lunch is served, my lady!" he announced cheerfully as he entered their bedroom.

Chloe looked up from the book she was reading, her face lighting up at the sight of him. "My hero!" she exclaimed joyfully with a chuckle. "What would I do without you?" As Cyrus settled the tray over her lap, she grasped his hand, her expression turning serious. "Cyrus, are you okay? You seem... I don't know... a bit distracted lately." She knew of no better way to say it.

For a moment, Cyrus felt tempted to unburden himself, to share the weight of his worries with Chloe. But seeing her face, etched with sadness from weeks of bed rest, he couldn't bring himself to add to her concerns. "I'm fine, love," he assured her, forcing a smile he truly didn't feel. "Just a bit tired. Nothing for you to worry about."

Chloe wasn't entirely convinced, but she nodded, squeezing his hand. "You're working so hard," she said, her voice thick with emotion. "I wish I could do more to help."

Cyrus leaned in, pressing a gentle kiss on her lips. "You're growing our baby. That's the most important job there is. Let me handle everything else." As he left Chloe to enjoy her lunch, he felt a twinge of guilt for his omission. They had always been open with each other, sharing their burdens and joys equally. But this time, he told himself, it was different. Chloe needed to concentrate on her health and the baby. He could manage the rest.

The afternoon flew by in a whirlwind of homeschooling lessons, household chores, and brief moments at his desk, attempting to extinguish fires at work. By the time evening arrived, Cyrus felt as though he had completed a marathon. After tucking the children into bed, he read their favorite stories, recited their nightly prayers, and then returned to Chloe. She was propped up in bed with a serene smile on her face, her hands resting on her belly.

"The baby's been active today," she said as Cyrus sat beside her. "Here. Feel." She guided his hand to a spot on her midsection, and Cyrus felt a strong kick against his palm. Despite his exhaustion, a wave of love and wonder washed over him.

"That's our little fighter," he said softly, his voice filled with awe. As they sat there, hands intertwined over the curve of Chloe's belly, Cyrus felt the day's tension begin to fade. This, he reminded himself, was what truly mattered. His family and the life they were creating together were all that mattered.

"Cyrus," Chloe said after a moment, her voice uncertain, "I... I've been thinking. Maybe we should reconsider hiring some help. Just for a little while, until the baby arrives and I'm back on my feet. I see how hard you're working, honey. You're running yourself ragged, trying to do it all. I feel so helpless, watching you struggle. We could use the help."

Cyrus gathered his wife into his arms, careful not to jostle her too much. "Oh, my love," he murmured into her hair. "You're not helpless. You're the strongest person I know." They held each other for a long time, drawing comfort from one another's presence. When they finally pulled apart, Cyrus felt a renewed sense of determination. "My family is worth the struggle, my love. As we always have, we will figure this out together—without any outside intervention. For now, rest. Prayerfully, tomorrow will come, and we will see things differently," he said, brushing a long braid away from Chloe's face.

As Chloe settled down to sleep, Cyrus retreated to his home office once more. The house was quiet, with the distant ticking of the grandfather clock in the hallway clearly audible. He stared at his computer screen, which was filled with dozens of unread emails and looming deadlines. The temptation to work through the night and attempt to catch up was strong. But he thought of Chloe upstairs, the baby growing stronger each day, and Cullen and Carmel sleeping peacefully in their beds. Taking a deep breath, he closed his laptop. The work will still be waiting for him tomorrow. For now, he needed to rest, recharge, and be the husband and father his family required.

As he climbed into bed beside Chloe, careful not to wake her, he sent up a silent prayer for strength, guidance, and the ability to navigate the challenges that lay ahead. Chloe stirred slightly, instinctively curling into Cyrus' side. He wrapped an arm around her, his hand resting protectively over her belly. At that moment, despite the worries still nagging at the edges of his mind, he felt a profound sense of peace. As sleep finally claimed him, his last conscious thought was one of gratitude for

Chloe, their children, and the life they had built together. It wasn't perfect or always easy, but it was theirs. And that, he knew, was the greatest blessing of all.

Chapter Five: Bridges of Understanding

The sprawling Victorian mansion loomed before Chloe as she pulled into the circular driveway, its imposing façade a stark reminder of the many tense visits she had endured in the past. But today felt different. As she helped Cullen and Carmel out of the car, smoothing down their Sunday's best clothing, she inhaled deeply, steeling herself for what she hoped would be a turning point in her relationship with Cyrus' mother. Chloe was grateful for this time away from home and out of bed, if only for a short while.

Mrs. Victoria Thornton stood at the top of the marble steps, her posture as regal as ever, but a softness lingered in her expression as she watched her grandchildren race up to greet her.

"Grandma!" Cullen and Carmel chorused, their excited voices echoing across the manicured lawn.

Victoria's face lit up with a warm smile—one that Chloe had seldom seen aimed at her. "My darlings!" she cooed, bending down to hug them. "How you've grown!" As Chloe approached the joyful trio, she felt a familiar knot of anxiety in the pit of her stomach, yet it loosened slightly when Victoria's gaze met hers. There was no hint of the cold disapproval she had grown accustomed to over the years. "Chloe, dear," Victoria said, her voice surprisingly warm. "Thank you for bringing the children. Please, come in."

The interior of the Thornton home was as opulent as Chloe remembered, but today, it felt less intimidating. Perhaps it was the sound of the children's laughter echoing through the high-ceilinged rooms, or perhaps it was the unexpected gentleness in Victoria's demeanor.

As the children dashed off to explore the garden under the watchful eye of the housekeeper, Victoria led Chloe to the sunlit conservatory. "I thought we could have tea here," she said, motioning toward a beautifully set table. "It's always been my favorite room in the house."

Chloe settled into a plush, cream-colored armchair, her hands instinctively resting on her midsection. The gesture didn't go unnoticed by Victoria, whose eyes softened even more.

"Cyrus told me the wonderful news," she said, pouring tea into gold-rimmed, delicate China teacups. "Another grandchild. I'm thrilled! Truly."

The sincerity in her words and voice caught Chloe off guard. "Thank you. We're... very excited."

Silence stretched between them, heavy with years of misunderstanding and tension. Victoria finally broke the deafening silence, setting her teacup on the saucer before her with a gentle 'clink.' "Chloe," she began, unusually hesitant, "I owe you an apology. Many apologies, in fact." Chloe's eyes widened in surprise. That was not how she had expected the afternoon to unfold. Victoria continued, her gaze steady yet filled with regret. "I've been... less than welcoming to you over the years. I had certain expectations for Cyrus' life, for the kind of woman I thought he should marry. I was wrong to judge you so harshly and try to interfere in your relationship."

Chloe felt her throat tighten as tears pricked at the corners of her eyes. "Mrs. Thornton, I—"

"Please," Victoria interrupted gently, "call me Victoria or Mom—whichever feels most comfortable for you. We're family, after all." That simple request was so long overdue that it nearly undid Chloe! She blinked rapidly, trying to maintain her composure. "I've watched you and Cyrus over the years," Victoria continued. "I've seen the love you share and the beautiful family you've built. The way you've supported each other through challenges and let faith guide your lives... I was too blind to recognize it sooner, but I see it now. You are exactly who Cyrus needs—who our family needs."

Chloe could no longer hold back her tears. They streamed down her cheeks as Victoria reached across the table to take her hand. "I'm so sorry, Victoria," she said, her voice thick with emotion. "I know I wasn't what you expected for Cyrus. I've worked so hard to be worthy of him and this family."

Victoria lovingly squeezed her hand. "Oh, my dear, you've always been worthy. It was I who wasn't deserving of the love and grace you've shown, even in the face of my disapproval."

As they sat there, hands clasped across the table, Chloe felt years of tension beginning to melt away. She reflected on all the times she had longed for Victoria's approval and the tears shed over cutting remarks and cold shoulders. Now, here they were, finally reaching an understanding. Their conversation flowed more easily afterward, touching on both painful and sweet memories. Victoria shared stories of Cyrus as a child, discussing how his stubborn determination and kind heart had been evident even then. Chloe, in turn, expressed her fears and joys as a mother, her passion for homeschooling, and her deep love for Cyrus.

Later in the afternoon, Cullen and Carmel burst into the conservatory, their faces flushed with excitement from their adventures in the garden. Victoria's eyes sparkled as she listened to their animated chatter, asking questions and laughing at their antics. Watching her children interact so naturally with their grandmother, Chloe felt a bittersweet ache in her chest. She had always hoped for a genuine family bond filled with unconditional love and acceptance.

And yet...

The weight of her secret bore down on her, threatening to shatter the newfound peace. As Victoria fussed over the children, admiring Cullen's latest drawing and praising Carmel's attempt at a cartwheel, Chloe felt a wave of guilt wash over her.

"Are you alright, dear?" Victoria asked, noticing Chloe's sudden pallor. "You look a bit peaky. Is it the pregnancy? Are you feeling okay?"

Chloe forced a smile, battling the nausea that had nothing to do with morning sickness. "I'm fine," she reassured her mother-in-law. "Just a bit tired, I suppose."

Victoria's brow furrowed with concern. "Of course. You must be exhausted. Pregnancy is no small feat, especially with two little ones to look after. Why don't you rest here for a while? I'd love to watch my grandchildren." The kindness in Victoria's voice only intensified Chloe's inner turmoil. How could she accept such warmth and care when she harbored a secret that could tear their small family apart?

As Victoria led the children out of the room, promising them cookies and stories, Chloe sank back into the chair, her hand once again instinctively moving to her belly. The joy of reconciling with Victoria was now tinged with deep, aching sadness. "Oh, Cyrus," she whispered to the empty room, "What have I done?" The tick-tock of the ornate clock on the mantel seemed to grow louder, each second a reminder of the truth she was suppressing. She closed her eyes, offering a silent prayer for strength and guidance.

When Victoria returned, Chloe had managed to compose herself, but the older woman's keen eyes didn't overlook the lingering sadness in her expression. "Chloe," she said softly, sitting beside her and taking her hand, "I hope you know that you can come to me with anything. Whatever burdens you carry, you don't have to face them alone."

For a fleeting moment, Chloe felt an urge to confide in Victoria, to unburden herself of the secret that was eating away at her, but she held back, knowing she needed to share it with Cyrus first. "Thank you, Victoria," she replied, squeezing the older woman's hand. "That means more to me than you know."

As the afternoon drew to a close and Chloe got ready to leave with the children, Victoria pulled her into a warm embrace. "Thank you for today. Thank you for allowing me the opportunity to make amends and be a part of your lives."

Chloe hugged her back tightly, fighting back tears. "Thank you for sharing your heart with us," she said. "It means the world to me."

Driving home with Cullen and Carmel excitedly chatting in the backseat about their day with Grandma, Chloe felt a complex mix of emotions. The increasing weight of her secret tempered the joy of reconciliation with Victoria. As she pulled into the driveway, she immediately noticed Cyrus waiting on the porch with a warm smile. At that very moment, Chloe decided she couldn't keep the secret to herself much longer. She would tell him soon—sooner than later, in fact. Whatever the consequences, she would confront them, and they would face them together.

He had promised her that.

Exhaling deeply, Chloe stepped out of the car, prepared to embrace her husband. Her afternoon with Victoria had revealed the strength of honesty and forgiveness. Now, she must summon the courage to apply those lessons to her marriage.

As Cyrus enveloped her in a loving embrace, he whispered, "Welcome home, my love."

Chloe held onto him more tightly than usual. Tonight, everything would change, but at that moment, surrounded by the love of her family, she found a glimmer of hope. No matter what storms lay ahead from revealing the truth, they would weather them together, just as they always had.

Chapter Six: The Secret Revealed

*L*ater that night, the glow of the bedside lamp cast long shadows across the bedroom as Chloe sat propped up against her pillows, her hands nervously twisting the edges of the blanket. Cyrus perched on the edge of the bed, his brow furrowed with concern as he studied his wife's face. "Chloe," he said gently, reaching out to still her restless hands, "what's wrong? You've been so distant lately. Please, talk to me."

Chloe's eyes, brimming with unshed tears that threatened to flood the room, met his eyes briefly before darting away. She took a shaky breath, her voice barely audible when she finally spoke. "Cyrus, I... I've done something terrible. Something unforgivable." The weight of her words lingered heavily in the air between them.

Cyrus felt his heart race uncontrollably as a cold, dreadful feeling settled in the pit of his stomach. "What do you mean?" he asked, his voice strained. "Chloe, no matter what it is, we can work through it. You know that. I promised you, and I meant it."

Chloe shook her head slowly from left to right, tears now flowing freely down her cheeks. "I'm not sure we can. Not this time. Cyrus, I... I... I betrayed you. I betrayed our marriage vows."

The world felt as if it were tilting on its axis as Cyrus processed her words. "Betrayed? Chloe... what are you... saying?" He knew he heard her, but did he truly understand her?

There was no turning back, so she forged ahead with her confession. "That night," she began, her voice breaking, "after our big fight about your mother... I was so angry, so hurt. I went for a drive to clear my head, and I... I ended up at Jake's place."

Cyrus flinched as if he'd been hit by a wrecking ball. Jake's name struck him like a physical blow. Jake, Chloe's ex-boyfriend from before they met, was the one she'd always claimed was "just a friend."

"Jake?" he repeated, his voice dangerously low. "What happened, Chloe? Tell me everything," he insisted.

Chloe's words spilled out in a rush, as if she couldn't bear to keep any of them inside any longer. "We talked, we had a little wine, and then we... Oh, God! Cyrus, I'm so sorry. It was just that one night, one terrible mistake. I've never, ever done anything like that before. I swear." She was having a full-blown meltdown.

Cyrus stood abruptly, pacing the room as he ran his hands over his hair. His mind was reeling, unable to reconcile the image of his faithful, loving wife with the betrayal she had confessed. "How could you?" he demanded, his voice rising. "After everything we've been through, everything we've built together, how could you throw it all away like that?"

Chloe reached out to him, her face a mask of anguish. "I don't know. I was weak. I was stupid. Cyrus, please, you have to believe me. It meant nothing, absolutely nothing."

He whirled on his heels to face her, his eyes blazing with pain and fury. "Meant nothing?! You slept with another man, Chloe! Your ex-boyfriend, of all people. How am I supposed to believe anything you say now?" As the full impact of her betrayal washed over him, a terrible thought struck Cyrus. His gaze dropped to Chloe's swollen belly, and he felt the blood drain from his face. "The baby..." he said, his voice hoarse. "Is it... is it even mine?"

Chloe's hands flew to her belly, her eyes wide with horror, saddened that he had made the possible connection so quickly. "I... I honestly don't know," she admitted, her voice a mere whisper. "The timing... it could be. But Cyrus, I swear to you, that was the only time I've ever—"

"Stop!" Cyrus roared, causing Chloe to flinch. "Just stop! How can I believe you? How do I know that was the only time? How do I know Cullen and Carmel are even—"

"Don't you dare!" Chloe yelled, her voice sharp with pain and indignation. "Cullen and Carmel are yours, Cyrus! I have never, ever been unfaithful before that night!" she cried out.

Cyrus laughed bitterly. The harsh sound changed the atmosphere of the room. "How can I ever trust you again, Chloe? Everything we have, everything we've built... it is all based on a lie!" he spat.

"No!" Chloe pleaded, struggling to sit up straighter in the bed. "Cyrus, please. Our love is real. What we have is real. Yes, I made a terrible mistake, but I love you and only you."

For a long moment, Cyrus stood silently with his back to Chloe, staring out the window into the darkness beyond. When he finally spoke, his voice was low and controlled, but it trembled with suppressed emotion. "I need to get out of here. I can't... I can't even look at you right now."

Chloe's sob tore through the room as Cyrus moved towards the door. "Cyrus, please!" she begged. "Don't go. We need to talk about this. We need to figure out what to do!"

He paused at the threshold, gripping the doorknob tightly. Without turning, he said, "There's nothing to figure out, Chloe. You made your choice that night. Now, I have to make mine."

With that said, he was gone, leaving Chloe alone in the suddenly vast and empty bedroom. She heard his footsteps on the stairs, followed by the front door opening and slamming shut, making the entire house shake. The roar of his car's engine soon faded into the distance. She collapsed back against the pillows as her body shook with each painful sob. How did it come to this? One moment of weakness, one terrible mistake, and everything they had built together crumbled around her.

As the night wore on, Chloe's mind raced with memories of their life together. The day they met at the church festival... their first kiss by the fountain in the park... the joy on Cyrus' face when she told him she was pregnant with Cullen. She thought of their wedding day and the vows they had made before God and their loved ones—vows she had broken in a moment of anger and confusion. She also thought of her children, sleeping peacefully in their beds, blissfully unaware that their world was falling apart. How could she explain this to them? How could they possibly understand?

As the first light of dawn began to creep through the windows, the baby within her stirred, as if sensing her distress. What if the baby wasn't Cyrus'? How could she bear to bring a child into the world under such circumstances?

Her heart sank when she grabbed her phone and saw there were no text messages from Cyrus. With trembling fingers, she typed a message:

"Cyrus, please come home. I know I don't deserve it, but please give me a chance to explain. I love you. Our family needs you. Please."

She hit the send button and waited, watching the screen with desperate hope. But as the minutes ticked by without a response, Chloe felt a cold certainty settle over her. Cyrus wasn't coming back. Not now, maybe not ever. That realization struck her like a ton of bricks, leaving her gasping for air.

This was real. This was happening. In one night, with one terrible decision, she had destroyed everything she held dear.

As the house began to stir with the sounds of a new day—Cullen's footsteps in the hallway and Carmel's sleepy calls for 'Mommy'—Chloe forced herself to sit up and wipe away her tears. She had to be strong for her children, if nothing else. As she swung her legs over the side of the bed, getting ready to face a world forever altered by her actions, she couldn't shake the feeling that this was only the start of a long and painful journey.

The road to forgiveness, if it existed at all, would be filled with obstacles. Trust, once shattered, was not easily rebuilt. As Chloe made her way downstairs to greet her children and begin the impossible task of honestly explaining why Daddy wasn't home, she prayed for a miracle that might somehow mend the hearts she had broken and save the love that once seemed unbreakable.

As she looked into Cullen and Carmel's innocent faces, their eyes wide with confusion and concern, Chloe knew that some wounds might be too deep to heal. The future that had once seemed so certain now stretched before her, a vast and terrifying unknown. All she could do now was confront it one day at a time, holding on to the hope that somewhere, somehow, love might find a way to overcome even this.

As the morning sun rose higher in the sky, casting its relentless light on the remnants of her perfect life, that hope seemed as fragile and elusive as a dream upon waking.

Chapter Seven: A Mother's Wisdom

The elegant sitting room of the Thornton mansion, once a symbol of cold formality to Cyrus, now felt like a sanctuary. He sat hunched over on the antique settee, his head in his hands. The weight of the past three days pressed down on him like a physical force. The revelation of Chloe's infidelity, the uncertainty about their unborn child's paternity, and the ensuing doubts about Cullen and Carmel had left him reeling, adrift in a sea of pain and confusion.

Victoria observed her son from across the room, her heart aching at the sight of his distress. She had never seen Cyrus so broken, not even during the darkest days of his rebellious youth. Silently, she crossed the room and sat beside him, her hand resting gently on his back. "Cyrus," she said softly. Her voice, filled with tenderness, still surprised her son. "Talk to me, darling. Let me help you carry this burden."

Cyrus lifted his head, his eyes red-rimmed and haunted. "How, Mom? How can anyone help with this? Chloe... she..." His voice broke, unable to finish the sentence.

Victoria nodded knowingly. Her expression was somber. "I know, my dear. Betrayal cuts deep, especially from the ones we love most."

"Love," Cyrus scoffed. The word tasted like the tartest lemon on his tongue. "How could she claim to love me and then do that? And now, to not even know if the baby is mine... How can I ever trust her again?"

His mother was silent for a moment, her gaze distant as though she were peering far into the past. When she spoke again, her voice was gentle yet firm. "Cyrus, there's something I need to tell you. Something I should have shared with you long ago."

Cyrus glanced at his mother, confusion briefly overshadowing the pain in his eyes. "What do you mean? Please don't tell me something like you're not really my mother! I couldn't bear that knowledge."

After taking a deep breath, Victoria began her story. "When I first married your father, we had a... challenging time. We were young, struggling to make ends meet, and the pressure was overwhelming. One night, after a particularly heated argument, I... I sought comfort in the arms of an old friend."

Cyrus stared at his mother in disbelief, struggling to reconcile the revelation with the image of the composed, proper woman he had known all his life. "Mother, are you saying...?"

Victoria nodded, her eyes glistening with tears that threatened to fall. "Yes, Cyrus. I was unfaithful to your father.

And when I found out I was pregnant shortly afterward, I was terrified. I didn't know if the baby—if you—were his or... or the result of my moment of weakness."

The room fell silent as Cyrus processed that information. His world, already tilted off its axis by Chloe's confession, seemed to shift once more. "Does... does Dad know?" he finally managed to ask.

"He does," she replied, her voice steady despite the pain evident in her eyes. "I told him everything, just as Chloe has told you. Admittedly, it nearly destroyed us, Cyrus. Your father left me for a week. During that time, I thought I had lost him forever. This was long before cell phones and texting existed. When he walked out the door, I had no way to reach him, especially not knowing where he went."

Cyrus experienced a sudden surge of anger, not just toward Chloe but also directed at his mother. "How could you keep this from me all these years? How could you and Dad pretend everything was perfect while holding onto this secret between you?" His world went from tilting to doing somersaults.

Victoria reached out, taking his hand in hers. "Because we chose to move past it. We decided to rebuild our love and our family. Was it easy? Of course not. We went through counseling with both our pastor and a professional. We had a paternity test conducted when you were born, which confirmed that your father was indeed your biological father. But even before we received the results, he had already made the choice to love you unconditionally, regardless of biology."

Cyrus stood abruptly, pacing the room as he had done so often in the past few days. "But how, Mom? How could he forgive you? How could he ever trust you again?"

"True love is stronger than our mistakes, son. This doesn't mean the pain disappears overnight or that trust is instantly restored. It's a choice we make daily to forgive, to heal, and to create something even stronger from the fragments of what was once broken."

Cyrus stopped pacing, turning to face his mother. "Are you saying I should forgive Chloe? Just like that?" He snapped his fingers on 'that.'

"No, not 'just like that,'" Victoria replied, rising to stand before her son. "Forgiveness is a journey, Cyrus, not a destination. What I mean is that you shouldn't rush to make decisions while you're consumed by pain and anger. Undoubtedly, Chloe made a terrible mistake, but one mistake doesn't erase years of love and devotion."

"But... the baby..." Cyrus began, his voice breaking.

Victoria placed her hands on Cyrus' shoulders, her gaze steady and compassionate. "The baby, regardless of biology, is innocent in all this. And Cyrus, think of Cullen and Carmel. They need their Daddy. They need their family intact."

Cyrus felt tears welling up in his eyes. The emotions he had held back for days finally began to break through. "I don't know if I'm strong enough, Mom. I don't know if I can face her again. How can I look at our children without wondering..." he said as his voice trailed off.

His mother pulled him into a tight embrace, her own tears falling freely now. "Oh, my darling boy. You are stronger than you know. And you're not alone in this. Your father and I will be by your side every step of the way. Whatever you decide, we'll support you no matter what." They stood there for a long moment, mother and son united in grief and love. When they finally separated, Victoria cupped Cyrus' face in her hands, her eyes filled with fierce determination. "Cyrus, I want you to listen to me very carefully. What Chloe did was wrong. There's no denying that. But I've seen how much that girl loves you. She transformed our family with her warmth and faith. One moment of weakness does not define her, just as it did not define me."

Cyrus nodded slowly, his mother's words beginning to penetrate the fog of pain and disloyalty that had clouded his mind for days. "But how do I face her, Mom? How do I look her in the eyes, knowing what she's done?"

Victoria's voice was gentle yet resolute as she responded. "With love, Cyrus. With the same love that has seen you through every challenge you've faced together. It won't be easy, and it won't happen overnight. However, if you both commit to healing and rebuilding trust, your love can emerge even stronger."

As the afternoon light began to fade, casting long shadows across the room, Cyrus felt a shift within himself. The pain was still there, raw and throbbing, but alongside it was a glimmer of something else—hope, perhaps, or the stirring of the deep love he had always felt for Chloe.

"I think..." he said hesitantly. "I think I need to go home to talk to Chloe, to... to try to understand."

His mother's face lit up with relief and pride. "That's my boy. Remember this, Cyrus: Love is a choice we make daily. Choose love. Choose your family. The rest will follow."

As Cyrus prepared to leave, gathering the courage to confront the uncertain future awaiting him at home, he turned to his mother one last time. "Thank you, Mom. For everything. I love you."

Victoria's eyes shone with tears as she embraced her son once more. "I love you, too, my darling boy. More than you will ever know. Now, go. Go home to your wife and children. They need you, and I suspect you need them, too."

Cyrus nodded in agreement, taking a deep breath as he stepped out into the fading light of the day. The road ahead would be complicated, fraught with pain and uncertainty. But as he drove home, his mother's words echoed in his mind, and he felt a flicker of hope ignite in his heart. "Love is a choice," she had said.

As he pulled into the driveway of the home he shared with Chloe, seeing the warm glow of lights in the windows,

Cyrus made his choice. He chose love. He chose his family. He chose the possibility of healing and forgiveness.

With a silent prayer for strength, healing, and wisdom, Cyrus stepped out of the car and walked toward his future, uncertain yet no longer alone in his pain. Whatever lay ahead, he would face it with the wisdom of his mother's words and the enduring power of love to guide him.

Chapter Eight: The Path to Healing

The yellow porch light cast shadows across the front yard as Cyrus' car pulled into the driveway. Inside the house, Chloe's heart raced—a mix of hope and fear coursing through her veins. She had spent the past few days in a haze of tears and regret, fervently praying for Cyrus' return.

As the front door swung open, Chloe rose from her seat on the couch in the living room, her hands instinctively cradling her swollen belly. Cyrus stood in the doorway, his face a mask of conflicting emotions: pain, anger, and, beneath it all, a flicker of the love that had brought them together.

"Cyrus," Chloe whispered, her voice trembling. "You came back."

Cyrus nodded slowly, his jaw tight. "We need to talk, Chloe. I mean, really talk."

They settled at opposite ends of the couch, the physical distance between them a stark representation of the emotional chasm that had opened up. Silence hung heavily in the air for a long moment, neither of them quite sure how to start the discussion.

Finally, Cyrus spoke in a low, strained voice. "Why, Chloe? How could you do this to us, to our family?"

Tears streamed down Chloe's face as she searched for the words. "Cyrus, I... I know there's no excuse for what I did. But I need you to understand: I never, ever intended to hurt you."

"But you did hurt me, Chloe," he said, his voice breaking with sadness. "You shattered everything we've built together into a million pieces. How am I supposed to trust you again? How can I look at our children—at this baby—without wondering?"

Chloe's hand moved protectively over her belly once more. "Cyrus, please. I know I've betrayed your trust, and I'll spend the rest of my life trying to earn it back if you allow me. But you must understand that my love for you and our family has never wavered."

Cyrus scoffed, the pain of betrayal evident in his eyes. "Love? If you loved me, how could you turn to Jake for anything? Of all people, Chloe—your ex-boyfriend? After all he did to try to destroy you?"

Chloe inhaled deeply, aware that her next words could make or break their future. "It... it wasn't about Jake, Cyrus. It was about me and the insecurities and doubts I've held onto for so long."

His brow furrowed in confusion at her words. "Insecurities? Doubts? What are you talking about? I've been faithful to you, Chloe."

"Rebecca," Chloe said softly, watching as understanding dawned on Cyrus' face. "I know it was years ago, and I thought I had forgiven you and moved past it. But the truth is, that moment of doubt, of wondering if I was truly enough for you... it never really went away."

Cyrus ran his hands down his face, frustration evident in the words that followed. "Chloe, nothing happened with Rebecca. Nothing. I told you that. How can you still doubt me after all this time?"

"I know, I know," she replied, her voice thick with regret. "It wasn't rational, Cyrus. It was my own insecurities and fears. That night, after our argument about your mother's interference, all those old doubts came flooding back. I felt so alone, so unworthy. As for Jake... he was just there."

Cyrus stood, pacing the living room as he absorbed the weight of his wife's words. "So, wait. Are you saying your infidelity was my fault? Because of something that didn't even happen years ago?"

"No!" Chloe exclaimed, rising to her feet. "No, Cyrus. This is on me. My actions, my mistakes. I'm not trying to excuse what I did. I'm just... I'm trying to help you understand." As her husband turned to face her, Chloe saw the conflict in his eyes. Anger warred with the love that still burned beneath the surface. She took a tentative step towards him, her voice soft but earnest. "Cyrus, you are the most incredible partner I could have ever asked for, and the most amazing father. What we have and what we've built together are lovely and precious. I know I've put that at risk and hate myself for it. But please, please believe me when I say you are the only man I truly love. You are the only one with whom I want to spend the rest of my life."

Cyrus' shoulders slumped, the weight of her words seeming to press down on him. "I want to believe you. God knows I do. But how can I? How can I ever look at you and our children and not wonder what other secrets you're hiding away?"

Chloe's heart ached at the pain in his voice. She moved closer—close enough to reach out and touch him, though she held back. "Cyrus, look at me. Really look at me." Slowly and reluctantly, he met her gaze. Her eyes were filled with tears, but they held a fierce determination that he recognized from the countless challenges they had faced together. "I know I've hurt you, and I understand it will take time to rebuild what we had. But Cyrus, you are the father of our children—all of them. Cullen and Carmel are yours without a doubt. Period. Full stop. And this baby," she placed a hand on her belly, "this baby is yours, regardless of biology—a product of our love, our family."

Cyrus' hand twitched, as if battling the urge to reach out and touch her belly. "But how can you be sure? How can we ever know for certain?"

Chloe took a deep breath, steeling herself for what she was about to say. "We can have a paternity test done, if that's what you need. But Cyrus, I want you to know this baby is yours, regardless of what that test might say. It's ours. If you'll have us."

The room fell silent as Cyrus processed her words. Chloe watched him, her heart in her throat, as he wrestled with the decision before him. Finally, after what felt like an eternity, he spoke.

"I don't know if I could ever forget what happened, Chloe. The pain. The betrayal. It's not something that simply disappears." Chloe nodded, her heart sinking. But before she could respond, he continued. "But I do know that I love you. Despite everything, despite the hurt, I love you. And our children—Cullen, Carmel, and this baby—deserve parents dedicated to one another and our family."

Hope blossomed in Chloe's chest as Cyrus stepped toward her. "Cyrus, are you saying...?" She needed him to be certain about his decision and hoped she understood him correctly.

He nodded, his eyes brimming with tears. "I'm saying I want to try to work through this and rebuild what we once had. It won't be easy, and I can't promise that things will ever be as they used to be. But I choose love, Chloe. I choose our family."

With a sob of relief, Chloe closed the distance between them, wrapping her arms around her husband. For a moment, he stiffened at her touch, but then his arms embraced her, holding her close. "I love you, Cyrus," she whispered into his chest. "I love you so much. And I promise, I will spend every day for the rest of our lives proving that to you."

Cyrus kissed the crown of her head, his voice thick with emotion. "I love you, too, Chloe. God help me, but I really do."

As they stood there, wrapped in each other's arms, both sensed the initial stirrings of hope. The road ahead would be long and tough, fraught with moments of doubt and pain. But at that moment, they silently vowed to face it together.

"What do we do now?" Chloe asked, gazing up at Cyrus with affection.

He met her gaze, a small smile tugging at the corners of his mouth. "Now, we take it one day at a time. We must be honest with each other, work on rebuilding trust, and love our children—all of them—with everything we've got."

Chloe nodded in understanding, her heart swelling with love and gratitude. "Together," she affirmed, her voice filled with determination.

"Together," Cyrus echoed, sealing the promise with a soft, passionate kiss.

As they stood in their living room, the couple felt the burden of the past few days start to lift. The journey ahead would not be easy, but they decided to confront it with renewed hope and commitment.

Their love story, tested by white-hot fire, was far from over. Instead, it was entering a new chapter—one of healing, forgiveness, and the enduring power of love to conquer even the deepest wounds. Guided by faith and strengthened by love, Chloe and Cyrus embarked on their journey to rebuild their family, stronger and more united than ever before.

Chapter Nine: A New Dawn

The morning sunlight filtered through the sheer curtains, casting an angelic glow on Chloe's face as she began to awaken. Beside her, Cyrus was already awake, his hand resting gently on her swollen belly. Their eyes met, and a small smile passed between them—a silent acknowledgment of the progress they had made and the challenges that still lay ahead.

"Good morning, my love," Cyrus cooed as he leaned in to plant a tender kiss on Chloe's forehead. "How are you feeling today?"

Chloe stretched carefully, mindful of her eight-month-pregnant body. "A bit achy, but good. The baby was active all night and this morning." As if on cue, a strong kick pressed against Cyrus' palm. His eyes widened in awe, even as apprehension flickered across his face. Those moments of connection with their unborn child had become precious to them, serving as reminders of the life they had created and nurtured together, regardless of the circumstances.

The past couple of weeks had been a journey of healing and rediscovery for Chloe and Cyrus. They had committed to rebuilding their relationship, brick by brick, with honesty and open communication as their foundation. It wasn't always easy, though. There were still times when the pain of betrayal would resurface, and doubts crept in like unwelcome houseguests. However, they faced each challenge together, clinging to their faith in God and the love that had brought them this far.

Their days settled into a new rhythm marked by intentional acts of kindness and understanding. Cyrus made a point of calling Chloe during his lunch breaks, just to check in and hear her voice. Chloe, in turn, left little Post-It notes around the house for Cyrus to find, reminding him of her love and commitment to their family. They had also begun seeing a Christian marriage counselor, Pastor David, who helped them navigate the complex emotions surrounding Chloe's infidelity and the uncertainty of their unborn child's paternity. The sessions were often difficult, compelling them to confront painful truths and long-buried insecurities. However, with each honest conversation, each tear shed, and forgiveness offered, they felt their bond growing stronger.

As Chloe's due date approached, the anticipation in their household grew. Cullen and Carmel were thrilled about becoming big brothers and sisters, their innocent enthusiasm soothing their parents' lingering anxieties. Cyrus devoted himself to preparing the nursery, painting the walls daisy yellow, and carefully assembling the crib. Each completed task felt like a step toward acceptance, a conscious choice to love this child unconditionally.

The night Chloe went into labor was a whirlwind of activity and emotion. As they rushed to the hospital, Cyrus held Chloe's hand tightly, whispering words of encouragement and love. The delivery room became a crucible of pain, fear, and, ultimately, joy as their daughter entered the world with a mighty cry.

"It's a girl!" the doctor announced, laying the squirming bundle on Chloe's chest.

Tears streamed down Chloe's face as she gazed at her daughter for the first time. "She's exquisite," she whispered, looking up at Cyrus with both love and apprehension.

Cyrus leaned in, his own eyes glistening with tears. As he studied the tiny face of his newborn daughter, his breath caught in his throat. A tuft of vibrant red hair peeked out from beneath the hospital cap, and when the baby's eyes fluttered open, he found himself staring into achingly familiar hazel orbs—but not from his own reflection. The room seemed to spin uncontrollably as the implications set in. Cyrus stumbled back slightly, his mind reeling.

Sensing his distress, Chloe reached out to grasp his hand. "Cyrus," she said softly, her voice shaking. "I... I don't know what to say."

For a long moment, silence hung heavily in the room, interrupted only by the soft coos of their newborn daughter. Then, with visible effort, Cyrus straightened his shoulders and moved back to Chloe's side.

"She's our beautiful daughter," he said, his voice thick with emotion. "No matter what, she's ours."

Chloe's eyes filled with fresh tears, this time of relief and gratitude. "I love you," she whispered, squeezing his hand tightly.

"I love you, too," he replied, leaning down to place a gentle kiss on both Chloe's forehead and their daughter's. "Both of you."

They named her Chelsea, which means "bright/shining." They had chosen the name together weeks before they knew the storm her arrival would bring. As they adjusted to life with a newborn, the joy of welcoming a new life was tempered by an undercurrent of uncertainty that flowed just beneath the surface of their interactions.

However, Cyrus stayed true to his word, showering Chelsea with love and attention. He embraced the responsibility of midnight feedings with determination, cradling her closely and singing soothing lullabies in the quiet hours of the night. Yet, Chloe couldn't miss the flicker of pain that crossed his face whenever Chelsea's hazel eyes, so much like Jake's, met his.

For Chloe, guilt was an ever-present companion. Each time she glanced at Chelsea's bright red curls, distinct from

Cullen and Carmel's dark locks, she felt the weight of her mistake anew. She immersed herself in motherhood with a passion driven by love and remorse, determined to be the best mother she could be for all three of her children.

Cullen and Carmel, blissfully unaware of the turmoil their parents were going through, doted on their baby sister. Their innocent love for Chelsea was a balm to their parents' wounded hearts, reminding them of the purity and unconditional nature of familial bonds.

As the weeks passed, the elephant in the room became impossible to ignore. The question of Chelsea's paternity loomed over the household like the darkest storm cloud, threatening to unleash its fury at any moment. It was Cyrus who finally broached the topic one night after they had put all three children to bed.

"Chloe," he started, his voice quiet but firm, "I think it's time we face this head-on. For Chelsea's sake, for our family's sake... we need to uncover the painful truth."

Chloe nodded in agreement. Her heart felt heavy yet relieved that the words had finally been said. "You're right. We can't continue living with this uncertainty. But Cyrus, I need you to understand this: No matter what the test shows, you are Chelsea's father in every way that matters."

He pulled her into a tight embrace and said, "I know. And I love her, Chloe. I love her so much it hurts. But we must do this. For all of us."

The next morning, Chloe called to schedule a paternity test. A few days later, as she and Cyrus waited in the DNA testing center's waiting room, with Chelsea cradled in her mother's left arm, the weight of the moment was overwhelming.

Cyrus reached out and took Chloe's free hand in his. "Whatever the results," he said softly, "we will face this together. As a family."

Chloe nodded, fighting back tears as she gazed up at her husband. In his eyes, she saw not only the pain and uncertainty of the past months but also the strength, love, and resolve that had carried them through. "Together," she repeated, squeezing his hand tightly.

When they were called into the testing room, Chloe and Cyrus shared a final look—one filled with fear, hope, and, above all else, love. Regardless of what the test results revealed, they understood that the true measure of family stretched beyond biology. It was found in the late-night feedings, tender kisses, and unwavering support through both joy and pain.

Chelsea, oblivious to the turmoil around her, cooed softly in Chloe's arms. Her tiny hand reached out, grasping Cyrus' pointer finger with surprising strength. At that moment, as they stood on the precipice of a truth that could change everything, Cyrus felt a surge of love for the little girl who had captured his heart from the second she entered the world.

Taking a deep breath, the couple stepped forward together, ready to face whatever the future might hold. Their journey was marked by challenges and hardships, but also by the enduring power of love and forgiveness. As they prepared to uncover the truth about Chelsea's paternity, Chloe and Cyrus clung tightly to the understanding that their family bond—formed through faith, tested by fire, and strengthened by unconditional love—was unbreakable.

The door closed behind them, signaling the end of one chapter and the start of another in the ongoing story of love, faith, and family. Whatever challenges lay ahead, they would confront them as they had confronted every other obstacle: together, with open hearts and an unwavering commitment to the family they had built.

Chapter Ten: Shattered Foundations

The envelope from the DNA testing center lay on the kitchen table, its crisp manila edges a stark contrast to the chaos it had unleashed. Cyrus stared at it, his mind replaying the moment he had ripped it open. His hands shook as he took out the single piece of paper inside. The words "PROBABILITY OF PATERNITY: 0.000%" in dark, bold letters on the pure white paper seemed to mock him, each letter a dagger to his heart.

Seven days had passed since that moment, yet the pain felt as fresh as if it were happening all over again. Cyrus moved through the house like a ghost, his body present but his spirit adrift in a sea of confusion and heartache. Chloe's voice, laden with tears, resonated in his mind: "Cyrus, please. I'm so sorry. I know this doesn't change anything, but I love you. We can get through this." But could they? He wasn't sure. He had asked for space, for time to process that life-altering detail. Chloe, filled with guilt and sorrow, had respected his wishes, giving him a wide berth as he wrestled with his emotions.

Now, as the soft cries of Chelsea drifted down from the nursery, Cyrus felt the familiar pull in his chest. Despite everything—despite knowing she wasn't his flesh and blood—he loved that little girl. It was a love tinged with pain and uncertainty, but it was love, nonetheless. He climbed the stairs slowly, each step feeling like a monumental effort. When he entered the nursery, he saw Chelsea squirming in her crib, her tiny fists waving in the air. Without thinking, he reached down and scooped her up, cradling her against his chest. "Shh. It's okay. Daddy's here," he managed to whisper with a trembling voice.

The word caught in his throat. Daddy. Was he still her Daddy? Could he be, knowing what he knew?

Chelsea's cries faded as she nestled against him, her warmth seeping into her father's skin. Cyrus gazed down at her, taking in her delicate features: the shock of red hair and the hazel eyes that were so unlike his own dark brown. How had he allowed himself to hope and believe when the truth had literally been staring at him in the face all along?

A fresh wave of anger suddenly washed over him. It wasn't directed at Chelsea but at the situation, Chloe, and himself for being so blind. He had promised to love this child unconditionally, regardless of biology. But now, confronted with the cold, hard truth, he struggled to reconcile his love for Chelsea with the pain of betrayal. He was lost in thought as he paced the nursery with Chelsea resting on his shoulder, when he suddenly heard the patter of little feet in the hallway. Cullen and Carmel appeared in the doorway, their faces aglow with innocence.

"Daddy, can we play with Chelsea now?" Cullen asked, his eyes wide with hope.

Cyrus felt a pang in his chest. Cullen and Carmel remained blissfully unaware of the turmoil affecting their family, seeing Chelsea only as their beloved baby sister. For them, family was simple: it was love, pure and uncomplicated. "Not right now, buddy," Cyrus replied, forcing a smile. "Chelsea needs her rest. Why don't you two go play in the backyard for a while?" As the children scampered off, Cyrus sank into the rocking chair with Chelsea still nestled on his shoulder. He began to rock gently, the rhythmic motion soothing both the baby and his troubled soul. "What are we going to do, little one?" he whispered. "How do we move forward from here?"

Chelsea cooed softly, her tiny hand clutching his shirt. As Cyrus gazed into her innocent eyes, he felt a surge of love so powerful it took his breath away. Biology aside, she was his daughter. He had been there since her first breath, holding and comforting her through countless nights, and he promised to protect and cherish her always.

But with that love came fear of the future and the challenges they would face. Would Jake, Chelsea's biological father, want to be part of her life? How would they explain this to Cullen and Carmel as they grew older? And what about his relationship with Chloe? Could they ever truly move beyond the betrayal?

As the days passed in the Thornton home, Cyrus found himself torn between his desire to protect his heart and his undeniable love for Chelsea. He had isolated himself from Chloe, interacting with her only when necessary, his words clipped and formal. Yet even in his pain, he couldn't bring himself to be cold toward Chelsea. Each night, after Chloe had gone to bed, he snuck into the nursery, spending time just watching baby Chelsea sleep and marveling at her tiny ten fingers and toes, memorizing every detail of her precious face.

Now, as Chelsea drifted off to sleep in his arms, Cyrus felt the weight of his decision pressing down on him. He knew he couldn't continue like this indefinitely. At some point, he would have to face Chloe to have the difficult conversation that would determine their family's future. Lost in thought, he didn't hear the soft footsteps approaching the nursery. It wasn't until he heard a sharp intake of breath that he looked up, finding Chloe standing in the doorway.

"Cyrus," she whispered, hesitantly stepping into the room, "I... I didn't mean to intrude. I just heard Chelsea crying earlier and wanted to check on her."

Cyrus nodded, unable to speak. He glanced down at Chelsea, peacefully asleep in his arms, then back at Chloe. The love he saw in her eyes for him and their children was unmistakable. But so was the pain and guilt that seemed to radiate from her very being. When their eyes met, something inside Cyrus broke. The walls he had built up over the past week crumbled, and he felt hot tears starting to stream down his face. He made no move to wipe them away, allowing them to fall freely as he held Chelsea close.

Chloe moved toward him slowly, as if she were approaching a wounded animal. When she reached the rocking chair, she knelt beside it, her hand hovering uncertainly near Cyrus' arm. "Oh, Cyrus," she began, her eyes filling with tears, "I'm so sorry—for everything. I love you and our family so very much."

Cyrus closed his eyes, feeling the warmth of Chloe's presence beside him. When he opened them again, he found himself looking directly at Chelsea's sleeping face. In that moment, he made a decision. It wasn't final, nor would it solve all their problems, but it was a start. "She's ours, Chloe. Chelsea is our daughter, no matter what that test said... no matter what... happened."

Chloe's hand found his, and she squeezed it gently. "Yes," she whispered. "Yes, she is."

They sat together in the quiet of the nursery. Cyrus held Chelsea while Chloe knelt beside them, both aware that the road ahead would be long and arduous. There were still conversations to be had, trust to rebuild, and wounds to heal, but surrounded by the love of their children, they found a glimmer of hope.

The love they shared—for each other, Cullen, Carmel, and yes, for Chelsea—was stronger than any test result, mistake, or moment of weakness. Chloe and Cyrus were united in their love, and although the path ahead was unclear, they would walk it together, one step at a time, guided by their faith and unwavering commitment to the family they had built with love.

Chapter Eleven: A Mother's Heart

Victoria and Cyrus sat across from each other in the elegant sitting room of the Thornton mansion. Victoria's face was a mask of concern and barely concealed pain as she listened to her son recount the recent events that had shaken their family to its core. "Oh, Cyrus," she said with exasperation, reaching out to take his hand. "My darling boy, I'm so sorry. I can't begin to imagine the pain you must be feeling."

Cyrus squeezed his mother's hand, grateful for her support. "It's been... difficult, Mom. But I love Chelsea. In my heart, she's my daughter, regardless of biology."

Victoria's eyes filled with tears. "Of course, she is. Love makes a family, not blood. But Cyrus, what Chloe did—"

"I know," Cyrus interrupted gently. "Believe me, I know. We're working through it for our family... for our children."

She nodded, her expression a blend of admiration and concern. "You're a good man, Cyrus. A better man than many would be in this situation. But I can't help worrying about you, about your heart."

They fell into a comfortable silence for a while before the sound of a car pulling up outside captured their attention. Cyrus glanced out the window and immediately recognized Chloe's vehicle. "I asked Chloe to join us," he explained, noticing the surprise on his mother's face. "I thought... I thought it was important for all of us to talk."

Victoria's posture stiffened slightly, but she nodded. "You're right. We need to address this as a family."

When Chloe entered the room, the tension was palpable. Her eyes were red-rimmed, evidence of recent tears, and she hesitated at the threshold.

"Come in, Chloe," Victoria said, her voice carefully neutral. "We have much to discuss."

As Chloe settled into her seat beside Cyrus, he reached out to grasp her hand—a gesture that caught Victoria's attention. The older woman's gaze softened slightly at that display of unity, even amid such chaos.

"Chloe," Victoria began, her voice steady but tinged with emotion," I need to understand: How could you do this to my son, to your family?"

Chloe's voice trembled as she replied. "Mrs. Thornton... Victoria... I know there's no excuse for what I did. I made a terrible mistake I'll regret for the rest of my life. But I love Cyrus, and I love our children—all of them—with all my heart."

Victoria's gaze was piercing as she studied her daughter-in-law. "Love? Is that enough, Chloe? Is it enough to heal the wounds you've inflicted?" Cyrus started to interject, but his mother raised a hand. "No, Cyrus. I need to hear it from Chloe."

Chloe inhaled deeply, squeezing Cyrus' hand for support. "You're right, Victoria. Love alone isn't enough. It takes work, commitment, and honesty... all the things I failed at when I made my mistake. But I'm committed to rebuilding what I've broken to earn back the trust I've lost."

Victoria remained silent for a long moment, her eyes distant as if lost in thought. When she finally spoke again, her voice was softer, carrying a pain that seemed to originate deep within her. "I once faced a similar situation regarding Cyrus' paternity. I've already discussed this with him, but I need you to understand, Chloe, that I grasp more about things than I sometimes reveal." She leaned back in her chair, gazing into the distance as if reliving the moment. "Mr. Thornton and I never informed Cyrus until recently. In the end, it didn't matter. His father loved him from the moment he learned of Cyrus' existence. We had a paternity test performed after his birth, which confirmed that Mr. Thornton was his biological father. But by then, it was irrelevant. Cyrus was his son. Period." She reached out, taking both Cyrus' and Chloe's hands in hers. "I'm sharing this with you now because I want you to understand something." She turned her attention to her son. "Cyrus, I defended Chloe before because I know firsthand how complex these situations can be. I know the pain, the fear, the doubt. But I also know the power of love and forgiveness." Turning to

Chloe, her expression softened, and she continued. "What you did was wrong, Chloe. It hurt my son and this family. But I see the love you have for him and your children. I recognize your remorse and determination to make things right."

The room grew quiet as Victoria's words sank in. Chloe's hands flew to her mouth, her eyes wide with shock and understanding regarding Victoria's confession. "I'm so sorry, Victoria, for everything. I never intended to cause so much pain," she replied tearfully.

Victoria nodded, her own eyes glistening. "I know, dear. And while it will take time to heal the wounds, I believe in the strength of this family and the love you two share."

As the three of them sat there, hands linked, the atmosphere in the room began to shift supernaturally. The tension that had been so apparent earlier quickly dissipated, replaced by a sense of shared understanding and cautious hope.

Cyrus glanced from his mother to his wife, overwhelmed with love and gratitude for both women. "Thank you, Mom, for sharing that with us and for your understanding."

Victoria smiled, genuine warmth shining through in her expression. "Family is everything, Cyrus. It's not always easy or perfect, but it's worth the fight."

Chole nodded. "It is. And I promise both of you, I will spend the rest of my days fighting for this family and our love."

As the afternoon went on, their conversation continued, touching on fears and hopes for the future. Victoria voiced her concerns about how they would address questions regarding Chelsea's paternity as she got older. Cyrus and Chloe outlined their plans to be open and honest with their children when the time was right, emphasizing the importance of love and family connections over biology. Throughout it all, there was an underlying current of love and support. Despite the pain and betrayal, there was also a shared commitment to healing and moving forward as a united family.

Before their departure, Victoria pulled both Cyrus and Chloe into a tight embrace. "We are family," she said firmly. "All of us, including little Chelsea. "We will face whatever comes our way together, with love and forgiveness guiding us." Despite their challenges, the trio genuinely believed that renewed hope was possible.

As the couple prepared to leave, Victoria pulled Chloe aside. "Chloe, I want you to know that while I'm deeply hurt by what happened, I also understand the complexity of human emotions. We've all made mistakes. What matters now is how we move forward."

"Thank you, Victoria, for your understanding and forgiveness. I promise to do everything I can to be deserving of both."

Victoria grabbed Chloe's hands and said, "Love, my dear. Love is what makes us worthy. Love for our children and love for our family. Hold onto that love. Nurture it, and let it guide you."

Baby Chelsea served as a reminder of the precious life to which they were all committed. In her, they saw not a symbol of past mistakes but a beacon of hope for a future built on love, forgiveness, and the unbreakable bonds of family.

Chapter Twelve: Truths and Choices

The small café buzzed with the mid-morning crowd, the clinking of cups and the murmur of conversations creating a backdrop for the tense silence at Chloe's table. Across from her sat Jake, his familiar features a painful reminder of the past and the reason for this difficult meeting.

"Thanks for coming," Chloe began. "This conversation won't be easy, but we need to talk."

Jake's expression was guarded. "What's this about, Chloe? Your message sounded urgent."

Chloe took a deep breath before speaking. "Jake, there's no easy way to say this, so I'm just going to be direct. Do you remember... that night... about a year ago?"

Jake furrowed his brow, then his eyes widened with recognition. "Chloe, we agreed never to talk about that again. It was a mistake. We both know that."

"I know, but something... happened as a result of that night. Something that changes everything." She reached into her purse and pulled out a small photo of Chelsea. With shaky hands, she placed it on the table between them. "This is my daughter, Chelsea." She paused for dramatic effect. "She's three months old, and... she's your biological daughter."

The color visibly drained from Jake's face as he stared at the photo. The shock in his eyes slowly gave way to disbelief and anger. "What? No! That's... that's not possible. We were careful, weren't we?"

Chloe shook her head, tears pricking her eyes. "Apparently not careful enough. I've had a paternity test done, Jake. There's no doubt. Chelsea is your daughter."

Jake leaned back in his chair, running a hand through his curly red hair. "Why are you telling me this now? What do you want from me, Chloe?"

"I'm telling you because you have a right to know," she replied, her voice steady despite the turmoil in her heart. "And because I need to know what you want to do about this. Chelsea is your biological child, and legally, you have rights—"

"Stop. Just... stop," Jake interrupted, holding up a hand. "I don't want any part of this, Chloe. I'm not ready to be a father. In fact, I never want to be anyone's father."

"I understand. Honestly, I was hoping you'd say that. Chelsea already has a father in Cyrus. He loves her, Jake. He's been there for her since the minute she was born."

"Good. That's... that's good. Look, Chloe. I'm sorry about all this. I really am. But I think it's best if I just stay out of it. Completely."

A mix of relief and sadness washed over Chloe. "I agree. Would you be willing to sign over your parental rights? To officially establish that Cyrus is Chelsea's father in every sense?"

Jake didn't hesitate. "Absolutely! I'll take care of any paperwork you need. Just let me know what to sign and when, and I'll get it done."

As they worked through the details, Chloe felt a tremendous weight lift from her shoulders. Although it wasn't the outcome she had envisioned when she first learned she was pregnant with Chelsea, it felt right. Cyrus was Chelsea's father. Period.

Before parting ways, Jake paused for a moment. "Chloe, I truly hope you and your family experience lasting happiness. I really do. However, I believe it's best if we don't see each other again after this."

Chloe fully understood the finality of his words. "I agree. Thank you, Jake, for everything." As she watched him walk away, she felt a chapter of her life closing. Now, she had to face the next challenge: telling Cyrus about her conversation with Jake.

The drive home seemed to stretch on forever. Chloe's mind raced with thoughts on how to approach the topic with Cyrus. When she finally pulled into their driveway, she saw him through the window, playing with Cullen and Carmel in the living room. Observing him so loving and attentive with their children gave her the courage she needed. "Cyrus," she called softly as she entered the house. "Can we talk?"

He looked up, sensing the urgency in her voice. With a quick word to the children to keep playing, he followed her into the kitchen. "What is it, Chloe?" he asked, his eyes searching her face.

"I met with Jake today."

Cyrus stiffened, his jaw clenching. "What?! Why?! What did he want?"

"He didn't want anything," she replied quickly. "I reached out to him because I thought... I thought he deserved to know about Chelsea. Plus, I wanted to understand what his intentions would be." She began to recount her conversation with Jake, observing the myriad of emotions that played across Cyrus' face: anger, hurt, relief, and finally, fierce protectiveness.

"So, he wants nothing to do with her?"

Chloe nodded. "He's agreed to sign over his parental rights. I made it explicitly clear that you are Chelsea's father. After all, you've been there for her from the beginning, loving her as your own."

Cyrus fell quiet as he processed the information. When he finally spoke, his voice was low and resolute. "I want to meet him."

"What? Why?" Chloe asked, surprised.

"Because I need him to understand something," he replied, his eyes blazing with intensity. "I need him to know that

I am Chelsea's father and will love and protect her with everything I have. I must make it clear to him—man to man—that he will never, ever have any influence in her life."

Chloe reached out, taking Cyrus' hand in hers. "Cyrus, you don't have to do that. Jake made his choice. He won't be a part of Chelsea's life."

"I know, but I need to do this for myself, Chloe. For us. For our family."

As they stood in the kitchen, the sounds of their children's laughter drifting in from the living room, Chloe felt a surge of love for the man who had chosen to love her daughter as his own. "Okay, if that's what you need to do, I understand. But Cyrus, please remember you are Chelsea's father. Nothing Jake says or does will change that."

Cyrus wrapped her in a tight embrace. "I know, and I promise to always be there for her, no matter what."

The next few days were a whirlwind of emotions and preparations. Cyrus insisted on meeting Jake alone, despite Chloe's concerns. She arranged the meeting, her heart heavy with the burden of the past and the uncertainty of the future. On the day of the meeting, Cyrus stood in front of the mirror, nervously adjusting his tie. Chloe approached him from behind, wrapping her arms around his waist. "Are you sure about this?" she asked softly.

Cyrus met her gaze in the reflection. "I'm sure. I need to do this for Chelsea. For us." As he prepared to leave, he paused by Chelsea's crib. The baby gurgled happily at the sight of him, her tiny hands reaching up. Without hesitation, he scooped her up, holding her close. "I love you, Chelsea," he whispered fiercely. "You are my daughter, and I will always, always be your father."

Chloe watched from the doorway, her heart swelling with love and gratitude. As Cyrus gently placed Chelsea back in her crib and turned to leave, Chloe saw the determination in his eyes. She knew then that no matter what happened at the meeting with Jake, Cyrus' love for Chelsea was unshakeable. "Go," she said softly, reaching up to kiss him. "Do what you need to do. We'll be here waiting for your return." As Cyrus drove away, Chloe prayed for strength, wisdom, and the love that had carried them this far to keep guiding them through whatever challenges lay ahead.

Chelsea might not share Cyrus' DNA, but she was his daughter in every way that mattered. Together, as a family, they would confront the future with hope, faith, and abundant love— qualities they would need for the days to come.

Will a trip to the hospital for baby Chelsea change everything, though? Their love, faith, and family security will soon be tested yet again.

Chapter Thirteen: Faith in the Storm

The sterile white walls of the hospital seemed to close in around Chloe and Cyrus as they sat in the small consultation room, their hands tightly clasped together. Dr. Patel, Chelsea's pediatrician, sat across from them, her face etched with concern as she delivered news that would shake their world.

"Mr. and Mrs. Thornton, Chelsea has Sickle Cell disease, and her condition is indeed serious. Our tests have shown that this is due to genetic factors," Dr. Patel stated, her voice gentle yet firm.

Chloe felt her heart drop as her grip on Cyrus' hand tightened. "Genetic... factors?" she repeated, her voice barely above a whisper.

Dr. Patel nodded, her eyes filled with compassion. "Yes. In cases like this, it's essential to have a thorough understanding of the child's biological background. It can offer valuable insights into potential hereditary issues and guide our treatment plan."

As the doctor continued to explain the intricacies of Chelsea's condition, which is prevalent in African American culture, Chloe's mind raced. She understood what this meant and where it could lead. The secret she and Cyrus had worked so hard to move past now threatened to resurface, bringing with it a storm of emotions and difficult decisions.

The drive home from the hospital was tense. The silence between them was filled with unspoken thoughts. It wasn't until they were in the privacy of their bedroom that the dam finally broke.

"We need to discuss this, Cyrus," Chloe said, her eyes pleading. "We may need to consider contacting Jake, for Chelsea's sake."

Cyrus's jaw tightened, his eyes flashing with pain and anger. "No," he said firmly. "Absolutely not. Jake made his choice. He's not a part of Chelsea's life, and I won't invite him in now."

"But Cyrus, this is about Chelsea's health. Don't we owe it to her to get all the information we can?"

Cyrus paced the room, running a hand through his hair in frustration. "Do you think adoptive parents have that luxury, Chloe? Many face these types of challenges and navigate their children's medical histories without direct access to biological relatives. We can do the same."

Chloe sank onto the edge of the bed, feeling defeat threatening to take over. "I know, I know. But this is different.

We know who Chelsea's biological father is. We can get the information we need."

"At what cost?" Cyrus demanded, his voice rising. "Do you really want to bring that man back into our lives? Into Chelsea's life? After everything we've been through?"

Defeat was knocking at the door loudly as Chloe remembered the pain in Cyrus' eyes when he learned of her infidelity and the long, difficult journey they had taken to rebuild their trust and family. She understood his reluctance and fear of reopening old wounds. "I don't want to hurt you. The Lord knows I don't want to jeopardize what we've built. But Cyrus, this is our daughter's health we're talking about. Don't we have a responsibility to do everything we can to help her?"

Cyrus turned to face his wife, tears welling in his eyes. "I am her father in every way that matters, remember? I've been there for her since the moment she was born. I've held her through every fever and sleepless night. How can you ask me to step aside and let Jake swoop in?"

Chloe stood and crossed the room to take Cyrus' hands in hers. "I'm not asking you to step aside, my love. Yes, you are Chelsea's father. Nothing will ever change that. But this isn't about us, Jake, or our past. It's about Chelsea and her future." As they stood there, she remembered the day they had stood before their family and friends, vowing to love and cherish each other through all of life's challenges. "Cyrus, do you remember what Pastor Merchant said at our wedding? About how our love should reflect God's love for us?"

"Yes, I do," he replied, his expression softening slightly. "He said that true love is selfless and that it always puts the needs of others first."

"Exactly. We made a commitment that day, not just to each other but to our family. To always do what's best for our children, no matter how difficult it may be," Chloe replied, her voice gaining strength.

They stood in silence for a long time, the weight of their decision hanging in the air like a helium balloon waiting to be popped. Finally, Cyrus spoke, his voice low and filled with sadness.

"You're right," he said, meeting Chloe's gaze. "Chelsea's well-being has to come first. But Chloe, I can't... I can't be the one to reach out to Jake. I just can't."

Chloe nodded, recognizing the pain behind his words. "I'll do it. I'll reach out to Jake and gather the information we need."

"Thank you, my love. This is all so difficult."

They held each other, drawing strength from their shared love and faith as peace enveloped them. They had made their decision, choosing to prioritize Chelsea's needs over their own fears and insecurities.

"We should pray," Cyrus suggested, pulling back to meet Chloe's gaze. Hand in hand, they knelt beside their bed, bowing their heads in prayer. Cyrus' voice, strong and steady, filled the room:

"Heavenly Father, we come before You now, humble and afraid. Our daughter, Chelsea, is ill, and we don't know what the future holds. Yet, we trust in Your plan, Lord. We believe in Your healing power. As it says in James 5:15, 'And the prayer of faith will save the one who is sick, and the Lord will raise him up.' We claim that promise now, Father. We ask for Your healing touch on Chelsea's body. Grant us wisdom as we make decisions about her care. Guide us, strengthen us, and help us to trust in Your perfect will for our lives. In Jesus' name, we pray. Amen."

As they rose from their knees, they felt a renewed sense of purpose and unity.

The next morning, as the first light of dawn streamed through the curtains, Chloe sat at the kitchen table, phone in hand. She had drafted and deleted countless messages to Jake, each endeavor feeling inadequate considering the seriousness of their situation. Cyrus walked into the kitchen, his eyes red-rimmed and tired-looking from a sleepless night. Without a word, he poured two cups of coffee and sat beside Chloe. His presence offered silent comfort and support. "I don't know how to do this," Chloe confessed.

Cyrus reached for her hand, covering it with his own. "Together," he said simply.

Taking a deep breath, Chloe started typing a message to Jake, asking for his help in gathering paternal information for Chelsea's medical care. When she pressed the send button, a wave of emotions flooded her: fear, hope, uncertainty, and, most importantly, a deep, abiding faith in their family's love for one another. She received a nearly instantaneous reply from Jake, and it wasn't at all what she had expected:

"LEAVE. ME. ALONE."

Each word was capitalized and punctuated by a period. That response finalized Chloe and Cyrus' option: With God's help and guidance, they would undertake this journey without Jake's assistance.

In the nursery, Chelsea stirred, her soft coos drifting through the baby monitor. Her parents exchanged a glance that reflected their swelling hearts, full of love for their daughter. As they rose to tend to her, Cyrus pulled Chloe into a tender embrace. "We've got this. God knew this would happen, and He will guide us through it," he whispered in her ear.

Chloe nodded, drawing strength from his words and the warmth of his embrace. Together, they walked toward the nursery, ready to face whatever challenges the day might bring, confident that their love, faith, and commitment to each other would help them through. They had weathered storms before, and with God's grace, they would endure this one, too.

Chapter Fourteen: A Family United

The steady beeping of medical equipment filled the hospital room as Chloe sat by Chelsea's bedside, gently stroking her daughter's tiny hand. The door creaked open slowly, and she looked up to see Cullen and Carmel tiptoeing in, their faces a blend of concern and determination.

"Mommy," Cullen whispered, his nine-year-old frame suddenly appearing older, "we brought you some coffee and a sandwich. Daddy said you haven't eaten all day."

Carmel, at seven, nodded solemnly while holding out a small white teddy bear. "And we got this for Chelsea. We thought it might make her feel better."

Chloe's heart swelled with love and pride as she watched her older children approach Chelsea's crib. They moved with gentle care that belied their youth. Cullen carefully placed the teddy bear next to his baby sister while Carmel softly hummed "Jesus Loves Me," a song they often sang at bedtime.

"Thank you, my loves. You're such wonderful big siblings."

Cullen puffed out his chest a little. "We're the Thornton Team! Right, Mommy? That's what Daddy always says. We stick together!"

Carmel nodded enthusiastically. "Yeah! And Chelsea needs us to be extra strong right now."

As Chloe observed her children interacting with their baby sister, she marveled at their empathy and love. It was a testament to the values that she and Cyrus had worked so hard to instill: kindness, compassion, and the importance of family.

Later that evening, when Cyrus arrived to take the night shift at the hospital, he found Cullen and Carmel setting up a small reading corner in Chelsea's room. They had brought a selection of their favorite picture books from home, eager to make the sterile hospital environment feel more inviting. "What's all this?" Cyrus asked, a smile tugging at his lips despite his fatigue.

"We're making it homey for Chelsea," Carmel explained with all seriousness, "so that she knows we're all here for her."

Cullen added, "And we thought maybe reading to her might help her get better faster. That's what you and Mommy always do when we get sick, right?"

Their father felt a lump rise in his throat as he pulled his children into a tight embrace. "Yes, that's right," he said softly. "You two are incredible, you know that?"

As the days went by, Cullen and Carmel remained a source of strength and support for their parents and little sister.

They took turns helping with household chores, ensuring there were always fresh flowers from their garden by Chelsea's bedside, and even organized a prayer circle with their Sunday school friends.

One particularly challenging day, when the doctors conducted more tests on Chelsea, Chloe was overwhelmed with worry. It was Carmel who noticed her mother's distress, quietly slipping her small hand into Chloe's. "Mommy," she said softly, "remember what you always tell us? 'God's got this. We just have to trust Him.'"

Chloe looked down at her daughter, struck by the wisdom in her young eyes. "You're right, sweetheart. Thank you for reminding me."

That evening, as Chloe and Cyrus sat in the waiting room on Chelsea's floor, stealing a few minutes alone while Cullen and Carmel sat with Chelsea, they reflected on their children's incredible resilience and maturity.

"They've been so strong through all of this," Cyrus mused, his voice filled with pride. "I can't believe how much they've stepped up for us and their little sister."

Chloe nodded, her eyes glistening with unshed tears. "They're embodying Proverbs 20:7 right before our eyes: 'The righteous who walks in his integrity—blessed are his children after him.' We've been blessed with such wonderful children, Cyrus."

Their alone-time was soon interrupted by laughter drifting down the hallway. Curious, they returned to Chelsea's room, where they found Cullen and Carmel putting on an impromptu puppet show for their sister. The sight of their children working together to bring a smile to Chelsea's face reaffirmed the strength of their family bond.

As they watched their children interact, Chloe and Cyrus felt renewed hope and determination. They had raised Cullen and Carmel to be compassionate, responsible, and loving siblings. Now, witnessing those qualities in action, they knew their family could tackle any challenge with grace and unity.

The weeks that followed would bring more tests, more sleepless nights, and more difficult decisions. But as Chloe and Cyrus stood in the doorway of Chelsea's hospital room, watching their older children shower their baby sister with love and attention, they felt a deep sense of peace. Cyrus pulled his wife close and whispered a prayer of gratitude for their beautiful family. They knew that with God's grace and their love, they could overcome any obstacle.

Their family was a testament to the power of love, faith, and unity—a living example of the blessings that arise from walking in integrity and instilling the same values in their children.

Chapter Fifteen: Growing Pains and Faithful Choices

The gentle autumn breeze rustled through the leaves of the old oak tree in the Thorton's' backyard, carrying with it the children's laughter. Cullen, now 12, was helping his 10-year-old sister Carmel perfect her cartwheel technique while their parents watched from the porch. Little Chelsea was nestled in Chloe's arms.

"They're growing up so fast," Chloe murmured, a hint of wistfulness in her voice. "It feels like just yesterday they were learning to walk. Look at them now."

Cyrus nodded, his eyes filled with pride and a touch of concern. "They're changing, that's for sure. And with those changes come new challenges."

As if on cue, Cullen jogged over to his parents, his face flushed with exertion and excitement. "Mom, Dad, guess what? John from church said there's going to be a science fair at his school next month. Can we go see it?"

His parents exchanged a glance, recognizing the familiar spark of curiosity in their son's eyes. It was a look they had noticed more often lately, especially when Cullen and Carmel's friends from church talked about their experiences at the local public school.

"We'll see, buddy," Cyrus replied. "Why don't you tell us more about it over dinner?"

At the dinner table that evening, the conversation inevitably turned to school. Carmel, her eyes bright with enthusiasm, chimed in, "Sarah said they're putting on a play at her school. She gets to be a tree! Wouldn't it be fun to be in a play, Mom?"

Chloe smiled, though her heart ached with a mix of emotions. "That sounds like fun, sweetheart. You know, we could create our own play here at home. Maybe we could invite your friends from church to join us."

Cullen's expression shifted slightly. "It's not the same, Mom. We always do everything at home or at church. Sometimes... sometimes I wish we could go to school like our friends do."

A heavy silence settled over the table. Chloe and Cyrus exchanged a look of understanding and concern. They knew this day would come eventually, but confronting it now felt daunting.

Cyrus cleared his throat, his voice gentle yet firm. "Cullen, Carmel, we've discussed this before. Your mom and I believe that homeschooling is the best option for our family. It allows us to ensure that your education reflects our faith and values."

"But Dad," Carmel protested, her lower lip quivering slightly, "we learn about God at church and at home. Can't we learn other things at school and still believe in God?"

Chloe reached out, holding her daughter's hand. "Of course you can, sweetheart. But it's more complex than that. Public schools aren't permitted to teach about God's love or integrate faith into their lessons. Your father and I want your education infused with God's Word and teachings."

Cullen, always the more analytical of the two, furrowed his brow. "But isn't that what Sunday school is for? We read the Bible every night as a family. Why can't we do that and still go to regular school?"

Those challenging and thought-provoking questions hung in the air. Cyrus inhaled deeply, silently praying for wisdom before speaking. "You both make valid points. Your mother and I understand your curiosity about public school, but our decision to homeschool isn't solely about religious education; it's about creating a learning environment that nurtures your entire selves—mind, body, and spirit."

As the conversation continued, Chelsea began to fuss, her tiny toddler face scrunching up in apparent discomfort. Chloe excused herself to tend to the little one, leaving Cyrus to navigate the increasingly emotional discussion.

"It's always about Chelsea," Cullen muttered, a touch of bitterness in his voice. "Ever since she got sick, everything's changed."

Cyrus' heart nearly skipped a beat at his son's words. He knew that Chelsea's ongoing health issues had placed a strain on the entire family, but hearing the hurt in his son's voice made the reality hit hard. "Cullen, Carmel, I know things have been different since Chelsea got sick. And I understand it's been tough on both of you. Your mom and I are so proud of how you've stepped up to help, but we also recognize that you might be feeling... left out sometimes."

Carmel began to cry. "We love Chelsea, Dad. We really do. But sometimes, it seems like you and Mom don't have time for us anymore."

The raw honesty of their children's words struck Cyrus like a physical blow from the strongest boxer on the planet. He pulled both of them into a tight embrace, his own eyes now stinging with unshed tears. "I'm so sorry," he whispered. "Your mom and I love you both so much. We never meant to make you feel neglected."

When Chloe returned, with Chelsea now calm in her arms, she took in the emotional scene before her. Without saying a word, she and Chelsea joined the family hug. For a long moment, they stayed that way, drawing strength and comfort from each other.

Chloe pulled away first and said, "We're a family. Families face challenges together. Your dad and I hear you, and we understand your desire to experience public school. We can't promise anything right now, but we want you to know that we're listening and take your feelings seriously."

Over the next few weeks, Chloe and Cyrus spent many nights engaged in deep discussions, weighing the pros and cons of public education against continuing to homeschool. They prayed fervently for guidance, seeking wisdom from their pastor and trusted friends who had faced similar choices.

One evening, as they sat on the porch swing, watching the sunset paint the sky in vibrant hues, Cyrus turned to Chloe with a heavy sigh. "You know, perhaps we need to consider that God's plan for our family might be different from what we initially thought."

Chloe nodded, her gaze distant. "I've been thinking the same thing. As much as I love homeschooling and believe in its benefits, I can't overlook the fact that Cullen and Carmel are craving something more."

"And with Chelsea's condition," Cyrus added, "maybe having the older two in school would allow us to focus more on her needs without them feeling excluded."

They sat in contemplative silence for a while, the weight of their potential decision hanging in the air between them.

Finally, Chloe spoke. "If we go through with this—if we send them to public school—we'll need to be even more intentional about nurturing their faith at home. We must have open, honest conversations about what they're learning and how it aligns—or doesn't—with our beliefs."

"I agree. We'll ensure they understand that their education at school is only one aspect of their learning," Cyrus remarked thoughtfully. "We'll keep teaching them about God's love and His Word here at home."

The next morning, Chloe and Cyrus called Cullen and Carmel into the living room. Nearby, Chelsea played happily in her playpen, blissfully unaware of the significant moment taking place.

"Your mom and I have been doing a lot of thinking and praying," Cyrus began, his voice gentle yet serious. "We've heard your desire to attend public school and have considered it carefully."

Cullen and Carmel sat up straighter, their eyes wide with anticipation.

Chloe picked up where Cyrus left off. "We want you to know that our decision to homeschool was made out of love and a desire to provide you with the best education possible—one that includes God's teaching in every subject. But we also realize that you're growing and changing, and your needs are also evolving."

"So, after much prayer and discussion," Cyrus said, "we've decided to enroll you both in public school for the upcoming semester."

The room erupted in a flurry of excited squeals and enthusiastic hugs. As the children celebrated, their parents exchanged a look of both apprehension and resolve.

"But," Cyrus added, once the initial excitement died down a little, "this decision comes with important conditions. We'll be very involved in your education and will have nightly discussions about what you're learning and how it relates to our faith."

Chloe nodded, adding, "We will continue having our family Bible study and prayer time. Your education at school is only one aspect of your learning. Our top priorities remain your spiritual growth and understanding of God's love."

The children nodded solemnly, fully understanding what their parents meant. "We promise to work hard and always remember what you've taught us about God," Cullen replied with sincerity in his voice.

That night, after tucking their children into bed, Chloe and Cyrus stood in the hallway. Their hearts were filled with love and hope for their family's future.

"We're doing the right thing," Cyrus whispered, drawing his wife closer. "It may not be what we originally planned, but I believe God is guiding us on this new path."

"You're right," Chloe replied, resting her head on his shoulder. "And who knows? This might open new opportunities for our family to share God's love with others!"

As they retired to their room, they felt a renewed sense of purpose and unity. They had faced numerous challenges in their journey as parents and knew more awaited them, but they were ready to embrace this new chapter in their family's story.

Chapter Sixteen: Faith Tested; Love Prevailed

Crisp autumn air nipped at Cullen's cheeks as he stood at the bus stop. Carmel fidgeted nervously beside him. It was their first day of public school, and despite the excitement that had bubbled within them for weeks after their parents decided to give public education a try, a tendril of apprehension now curled in the pit of their stomachs.

"Remember," Cullen said, squeezing Carmel's hand, "Mom and Dad told us to be ourselves and let God's love shine through us."

Carmel nodded, her long, curly pigtails bouncing in unison. "And to make new friends!" she exclaimed happily.

When the long yellow bus filled with rambunctious children rumbled to a stop before them, Cullen took a deep breath. "Here we go," he murmured, more to himself than to Carmel. "A new adventure."

The first few weeks of school were a whirlwind of new experiences. Cullen and Carmel marveled at the bustling hallways, the variety of subjects taught by different teachers, and the energy of so many children learning together. They immersed themselves in their studies with enthusiasm, eager to show their parents that they could thrive in this new environment.

It was during lunch on a Wednesday when Cullen first felt the sting of his peers' ridicule. He bowed his head to say grace before eating, a habit ingrained since childhood. A group of boys at the next table noticed. "Hey, look!" one of them teased. "The new kid's talking to his imaginary friend!" Laughter rippled through the cafeteria, and Cullen felt his cheeks burn with embarrassment. He looked up to see Carmel at another table, her eyes wide with concern for her big brother.

That incident marked the start of a challenging journey for the Thornton children. As they sought to share their faith and the love of God that had been fundamental to their upbringing, they encountered skepticism, mockery, and occasionally, outright hostility.

Carmel faced her own difficulties on the playground. When she suggested playing "Noah's Ark" during recess—a game she and Cullen had often enjoyed at home—her classmates scoffed. "That's just a made-up story," a girl named Lily declared. "My mom says the Bible is just a book full of fairytales."

Carmel's heart sank. "But it's not," she protested weakly. "It's God's Word, and it's true." The other girls exchanged glances and giggled, leaving Carmel standing alone by the swings, fighting back tears.

As time passed, the bullying intensified. Cullen discovered cruel notes shoved into his locker, ridiculing his faith and labeling him a "Jesus Freak." Carmel overheard murmurs in the girls' bathroom—other students scheming to exclude her from birthday parties because she was "too weird" with all her talk about her imaginary God.

At home, their parents noticed the change in their children. Cullen, once outgoing and quick to share stories about his day, became increasingly withdrawn. Carmel's usual bubbly demeanor transformed to quiet introspection.

One evening, as Chloe tucked Carmel into bed, her daughter finally broke down. "Mommy," she sobbed, "why don't they like us? We're just trying to be nice and share God's love, just like you and Daddy taught us."

Chloe's heart shattered as she held Carmel close. "Oh, sweethcart," she replied, stroking her daughter's hair. "Sometimes, people are afraid of what they don't understand. But that doesn't mean you've done anything wrong."

Meanwhile, Cyrus found Cullen sitting alone in the backyard, gazing at the stars. "Do you want to talk about it, buddy?" he asked gently, settling beside his son.

Cullen was quiet for a long time before speaking. "Dad, is it wrong to believe in God? To want to share His love with others?" he asked with a sigh.

Cyrus felt a lump form in his throat. "No, son," he said firmly. "It's not wrong at all. In fact, it's one of the most important things we can do as Christ's disciples. But sometimes, the world doesn't understand or accept that."

As the children's struggles at school became more apparent and frequent, their parents agonized over what to do. They had wanted their children to experience the world beyond their homeschool bubble, make new friends, and learn in a different environment. They hadn't anticipated the harsh reality of a world that often rejects the values they hold dear.

After three months of watching their children's spirits dim, Chloe and Cyrus made the difficult decision to unenroll them from public school. The night they broke the news to them, emotions ran high in the Thornton household.

"We're so proud of both of you," Cyrus began. "You've demonstrated incredible strength and courage in standing up for your beliefs at school."

Chloe nodded, adding, "But we can't just stand by and watch you suffer. We believe bringing you back home for your education is the best option for now."

To their surprise, both children appeared relieved. "I tried, Mom and Dad," Cullen said quietly. "I really did, but it was so hard."

Carmel's lower lip trembled as she said, "I just wanted to make new friends, but nobody wanted to be friends with the 'weird Christian girl.'"

Chloe and Cyrus frequently exchanged concerned glances, questioning whether they had made the right decision in sending their children to public school in the first place. Once they settled back into the rhythm of homeschooling, Chloe and Cyrus worked tirelessly to rebuild their children's confidence and reaffirm their faith. They organized playdates with other homeschooling families and encouraged Cullen and Carmel to maintain friendships with the children from the church.

Unfortunately, the scars from their public school experience ran deep, especially for Cullen. He grew more reserved, spending long hours alone in his room with his books, lost in thought. One sunny afternoon, while Cullen sat on the porch swing, once again lost in thought, he felt a small hand tugging at his sleeve. He looked down to see Chelsea, her eyes wide and curious. "Cull-Cull sad?" she asked, her little brow furrowed in concern.

Before he could respond, Carmel appeared, her face set with determination. "Come on, Cullen," she said, taking his hand. "We're all going on an adventure!" Despite his reluctance, Cullen allowed himself to be pulled along by his sisters. They led him to the old treehouse in the backyard—the place that had once been his favorite hideaway. Carmel had created a makeshift picnic inside, featuring peanut butter and jelly sandwiches, banana slices, and fresh lemonade. "We're having a special Sibling Day!" she announced, her eyes shining with love for her brother.

As the trio sat in the treehouse, sharing sandwiches and stories, Cullen felt something shift within him. The love of his family, unconditional and unwavering, began to soothe the hurt he had been carrying.

From the kitchen window, their parents watched them interact and play, tears glistening in their eyes. "We've made mistakes," Chloe whispered, leaning into her husband's embrace, "but look at them. They're resilient. They have each other."

Cyrus tightened his arm around Chloe and said, "And they have us. We'll get through this together, as a family."

As the sun began to set, Cullen stepped out of the treehouse with Chelsea perched on his shoulders and Carmel by his side. For the first time in months, a genuine smile lit up his face. Their parents rushed out to meet them, enveloping their children in a group hug. In that moment, surrounded by the love of his family, Cullen felt a flicker of hope reignite in his heart. The world might not always understand or accept their faith, but here, in the safety of their home and the strength of their family bond, he knew they could face anything. "I love you guys," he said softly, his voice muffled against his father's shoulder.

"We love you, too, sweetheart," Chloe replied, her voice thick with emotion. "Always and forever."

Bathed in the warm glow of the setting sun, the Thornton family reaffirmed their commitment to each other and their faith. They had weathered yet another storm, and although there would undoubtedly be more, they faced the future with renewed strength and unwavering love. The experience had taught them valuable lessons about the complexities of the world, the importance of staying true to one's beliefs, and the unbreakable bond of family.

As they walked back into the house hand in hand, they carried with them the understanding that, no matter what challenges they might face, their love for one another and their faith in the One True God would guide them through.

Chapter Seventeen: Love Tested; Love Triumphant

C andlelight flickered across Chloe and Cyrus's faces as they sat with their new friends, William and Wendy, at La Petite Maison. The French bistro had been a favorite of theirs for years, a place where they had shared countless moments of joy and heartache throughout their relationship.

"Here's to new friendships!" William toasted, raising his glass of white wine. The others followed suit, clinking their glasses as laughter filled the air.

Chloe couldn't help but notice how Wendy's eyes lingered on Cyrus. Her smile was just a touch too bright, her laughter a bit too enthusiastic at his witticisms. A familiar twinge of unease settled in the pit of her stomach, but she pushed it aside, determined to enjoy the evening.

As the weeks passed, the two couples fell into a comfortable rhythm of double dates and shared activities. They explored art galleries, tried new restaurants, and even joined a couple's bowling league at their church. Chloe genuinely enjoyed William's company. His dry humor and thoughtful insights reminded her of her father. However, Wendy's behavior towards Cyrus continued to gnaw at her. It was in the little things—a lingering touch on his arm, how she always managed to sit next to him at group gatherings, the inside jokes they seemed to be developing...

One evening, as they got ready for bed after another night out with William and Wendy, Chloe couldn't contain her concern any longer. "Cyrus," she started nervously, "have you noticed anything... strange about Wendy?"

Cyrus looked up from setting the alarm clock, his brow furrowed in confusion. "Strange? What do you mean?"

Chloe sighed as she sank onto the edge of the bed. "The way she acts around you is... well, it's flirtatious, Cyrus. And it makes me uncomfortable."

Cyrus' eyes widened in utter surprise. "Flirtatious? Chloe, I think you're reading too much into it. Wendy's just friendly, that's all." Yet, as he saw the hurt in his wife's eyes, memories of their past struggles flooded his mind: the pain of his near-indiscretion with Rebecca, Chloe's infidelity with Jake, the challenges they faced with Chelsea's paternity and health—it all came rushing back in a wave of emotion that nearly knocked him off his feet. "Oh, my love. I'm sorry. I didn't realize it was bothering you so much. But you must know, nothing is going on between her and me. You're the only woman for me, Chloe. You always have been and always will be."

Chloe leaned into his embrace, drawing comfort from his familiar warmth. "I know that. I do. It's just... after everything we've been through, I can't help but worry sometimes."

He pulled back slightly, locking eyes with her in fierce intensity. "Then let's put those worries to rest. We can stop hanging out with William and Wendy entirely if it makes you uncomfortable. Your peace and happiness are far more important than any double date."

"No, love. That's too extreme. They're our friends, and I genuinely enjoy spending time with them. I just... I need you to make it clear to Wendy that you're a happily married man. Can you do that for me?"

He nodded without hesitation. "Of course. Anything for you, sweetheart."

The next time they met up with William and Wendy, Cyrus intentionally showed more affection toward Chloe, holding her hand and stealing kisses throughout the evening. He also made several pointed remarks about their happy marriage and the strength of their family. Wendy's reaction was subtle yet unmistakable. Her smile became slightly forced, and her laughter was a bit too loud. By the end of the night, there was palpable tension in the air.

A few days later, Chloe received an unexpected text message from Wendy:

"I think it's best if we take a step back from our friendship. Things have gotten complicated. I'm sorry."

When Chloe showed the message to Cyrus, his surprise and hurt were evident. "I'm sorry, Chloe. You were obviously right about Wendy. I should have seen it sooner," he admitted.

She wrapped her arms lovingly around her husband's waist. "No, Cyrus. You did exactly what I asked. You showed her that our marriage is strong and that we're committed to each other. That's all that matters." As they stood in the kitchen, holding each other close, she felt a renewed appreciation for the depth of their love. They were still standing, still loving, and still choosing each other every day.

"You know, maybe this was a good reminder for us never to take what we have for granted. We must keep choosing each other and working on our relationship every single day," Cyrus stated.

"You're right. And maybe we need to make more time for just us. Date nights, weekend getaways… time to reconnect and remember why we fell in love in the first place."

Cyrus looked at Chloe with a mischievous glint in his eyes. "Well, Mrs. Thornton, how about we start right now? The children are in bed, and the kitchen is clean. "How about we have our own little date night right here at home?"

Chloe laughed, the sound light and carefree. "I'd say that sounds perfect, Mr. Thornton."

They settled onto the sofa with a bottle of Petrolo Galatrona—a red wine they had saved for a special occasion—

and turned on their favorite movie, savoring their alone time without any outside distractions.

The loss of their friendship with William and Wendy served as a reminder that not all relationships are meant to last. It also strengthened the bond between Chloe and Cyrus, highlighting the precious gift they had in each other. As the movie continued playing, mostly ignored in favor of stolen kisses and whispered conversations, they reaffirmed their commitment to one another. They discussed their dreams for the future, their hopes for their children, and their gratitude for the life they had built together.

"I love you, Cyrus Thornton. More than yesterday."

"And I love you, Chloe Thornton. Forever and always."

As they drifted off to sleep that night, tangled in each other's arms, both felt a renewed sense of purpose and unity. They had faced yet another test of their love and emerged even stronger for it.

The next morning, as they gathered around the breakfast table with their children, Chloe and Cyrus exchanged a glance filled with deep understanding and love. This was what mattered most: their family, their faith, and the unbreakable bond they shared. Everything else was merely noise, unable to penetrate their fortress of love. The best chapters of their lives were yet to be written, and they were ready for them.

Chapter Eighteen: From the Ashes, Hope Rises

The glow of candlelight flickered in the living room, casting dancing shadows on the walls. Chloe and Cyrus sat cuddled on the couch, relishing a rare moment of peace and quiet in their bustling household. A comfortable silence enveloped them as the children slept upstairs.

Cyrus pressed a soft kiss to Chloe's temple. "I love nights like this—just you and me, no distractions."

Chloe hummed in agreement, nestling closer. "It's perfect," she whispered.

The tranquility of the moment was shattered by a sudden, piercing scream from upstairs. "Fire! Fire!"

In an instant, Chloe and Cyrus were on their feet, hearts pounding. The acrid smell of smoke filled the air as they raced towards the stairs. Flames licked at the hallway walls, emanating from Cullen's room. "Cullen!" Cyrus shouted, his voice hoarse with fear. "Carmel! Chelsea!" Without hesitation, he plunged into the smoke-filled hallway, heading straight for Cullen's room.

Chloe, fighting back panic, rushed to the girls' room.

"Mommy!" Carmel cried, clutching a terrified Chelsea to her chest.

"Come on, babies," Chloe urged, scooping up Chelsea and grabbing Carmel's hand. "We need to get out. Right now!"

The heat was intense, and the smoke thickened with each passing second. Chloe guided her daughters down the stairs, her eyes stinging and her lungs burning. She silently prayed for Cyrus and Cullen's safety. Once outside, the cool night air shocked their systems. Chloe set Chelsea down and pulled both girls close as they watched the flames engulf their home. Neighbors began to emerge from their houses, drawn by the commotion and the ominous orange glow.

"Cyrus... Cullen," Chloe whispered, her gaze fixed on the front door. "Please, God. Let them be okay." As if in response to her prayer, Cyrus burst through the door, cradling Cullen in his arms. Both were coughing violently, their faces streaked with soot. Chloe rushed to them, tears streaming down her face. "Oh, thank God," she sobbed, embracing them tightly. "Thank God you're safe."

The family of five huddled together on the front lawn, watching helplessly as the firefighters arrived and battled the blaze. The crackling flames and gray ashes floating toward them punctuated the crash of their collapsing home. Everything they owned, every cherished memory held within those walls, was being reduced to debris before their eyes.

Neighbors gathered around them, offering blankets, words of comfort, and silent support. Mr. and Mrs. Thompson, the elderly couple next door, approached with tears in their eyes. "Oh, you poor dears," Mrs. Thompson said, her voice trembling. "You'll stay with us for as long as you need. We have plenty of room."

Cyrus nodded gratefully. "Thank you," he managed to say through another lung-cleansing cough. "We... we don't know what to say."

As the fire slowly died down, leaving behind the skeletal remains of their home, the reality of their situation began to sink in. They had lost everything—clothing, furniture, photos, keepsakes... But as Chloe looked at her family, all safe and whole, she felt a surge of gratitude amid the grief. "We're alive," she whispered, squeezing Cyrus' hand. "We're alive, and we're together. That's what matters the most."

"You're right," Cyrus agreed. "We have each other. We'll get through this."

The days that followed were a blur of insurance claims, donations, and adapting to life in the Thompsons' guest rooms. The community came together, offering clothes, toys for the children, and an abundance of casseroles. Their church organized a fundraiser to help them regain their footing.

Despite the overwhelming support, the emotional toll was significant. Cullen became distant, haunted by nightmares of the fire. Carmel grew clingy, refusing to let her parents out of her sight. Even little Chelsea seemed to sense the disruption, her typically sunny disposition replaced by anxiety.

One evening, about a week after the fire, Chloe found Cyrus sitting alone on the Thompsons' back porch, staring off into the distance. She settled beside him and took his hand in hers. "What's on your mind, love?" she asked softly.

"I keep thinking about everything we lost due to an electrical fire," he admitted. "The photo albums, the children's baby books, your grandmother's quilt... It's all gone, Chloe. Many things can't be replaced. How do we move forward from here?" He let out a heart-wrenching sigh.

She leaned on his shoulder, carefully considering her words. "We move forward the same way we always have," she said at last. "Together, with faith in God's plan for us. Yes, we've lost things—precious things. But we have our memories and our love for each other. And, most importantly, we have our family, safe and sound."

Cyrus turned to look at her, a small smile tugging at his lips. "How do you always know exactly what to say?"

Chloe shrugged and returned his smile. "It's a gift," she teased, before becoming serious again. "But Cyrus, I mean it. This is just another test of our faith and love." As if to underscore her words, the sound of laughter drifted through the open living room window. Cullen and Carmel were playing a board game with Mr. Thompson. Their giggles were a balm to their parents' weary souls.

"You're right," Cyrus said, pulling his wife close. "We'll rebuild and make new memories. And we'll do it together."

In the following weeks, the Thornton family gradually started to heal. Cullen's nightmares became less frequent, and Carmel's clinginess subsided. They settled into a routine with the Thompsons, assisting with chores and sharing meals. It wasn't perfect, but they made the most of it, discovering moments of joy and laughter amidst the daily struggles.

One Sunday morning, as they prepared for church, Chloe overheard Cullen talking to Carmel. "You know," he said, his voice thoughtful, "I was really sad about losing all my things in the fire, but then I realized something: All that stuff? It's just stuff. What really matters is that we're all okay." Chloe felt tears prick her eyes at her son's words. She caught Cyrus' gaze across the room, seeing her own emotions reflected there. Their children were resilient, learning valuable lessons about what truly mattered in life.

At church that day, Pastor Merchant's sermon felt tailor-made for their situation. He spoke about rising from the ashes and how God can bring beauty from destruction. "In our darkest moments," he said, his voice ringing out across the congregation, "when we feel we've lost everything, that's when God's light shines the brightest. He is always with us, ready to help us rebuild, not just our physical surroundings but our spirits as well."

As they listened with their hands clasped tightly together, Chloe and Cyrus felt a renewed sense of hope. Yes, they had lost their home and possessions, but they had gained a deeper appreciation for what truly mattered: their faith, family, and the love that bound them, always and forever.

That evening, as they gathered around the Thompsons' dining table for dinner, Cyrus cleared his throat. "I have an announcement to make," he said, a hint of excitement in his voice. "I've been talking with the insurance company, and we've finally settled on a payout. It's enough... it's enough for us to start rebuilding our home bigger and better than before!" he finished with great enthusiasm.

The room erupted with cheers and excited chatter. As Chloe looked at her children—Cullen's eyes shining with hope, Carmel bouncing happily in her seat, and Chelsea giggling at all the excitement—she felt a powerful surge of love and gratitude wash over her. "We're going to be okay," she whispered to Cyrus, squeezing his hand under the table.

"More than okay. We're going to be stronger than ever."

Soon, they started planning their new home, incorporating ideas from every family member. Chloe and Cyrus marveled at how this tragedy had drawn them closer together. Yes, they lost material possessions, but they gained so much more: a deeper appreciation for one another, a stronger faith, and the understanding that they could weather any storm as long as they faced it together.

The road ahead would not be easy. They would face challenges and setbacks as they rebuilt their home and lives. However, while standing on the empty lot where their old house had once stood, envisioning the new home that would rise in its place, Chloe and Cyrus felt a sense of peace and excitement about the future.

"From these ashes of a life that once was, we'll build something magnificent," Cyrus said, his arm around Chloe's waist. "It will be a testament to God's grace and the strength of our love."

"Yes, a new chapter in our story," she agreed. "One filled with hope, faith, and endless love."

The Thornton family stood united as the sun set on that promise-filled day, casting a heavenly golden glow over the land that would soon hold their new home. They had faced the fire and emerged as survivors—stronger, more faithful, and more in love than ever. Their love story was still being written, one day at a time.

Chapter Nineteen: Rising From the Ashes

The early morning sun streamed through the windows of Mr. and Mrs. Thornton's guest bedroom, gently waking Chloe from her slumber. For a moment, confusion clouded her mind as she took in her unfamiliar surroundings. Then, as it had every morning for the past few weeks, reality set in: their home was gone, reduced to ashes by a merciless fire. Yet, as she turned to see Cyrus sleeping peacefully beside her, a wave of gratitude washed over her. She was thankful for her mother-in-law's gracious offer to have the family move in with them, easing any burden on the Thompsons. "Thank You, Lord, for keeping us safe, giving us shelter, and for Your endless love," she whispered as she looked up toward Heaven.

As if sensing her stirring, Cyrus' eyes fluttered open. He reached for her hand, intertwining their fingers. "Good morning, love," he said, his voice still thick with sleep. "How are you feeling today?"

"Grateful. Always grateful," she replied.

Their morning routine had changed significantly since moving in with Cyrus' parents, but they found solace in the new rhythms they had established. As the couple descended the stairs, the aroma of freshly brewed coffee greeted them. In the kitchen, they found Victoria already bustling about, preparing breakfast.

"Good morning, dears," Victoria chirped, her eyes crinkling warmly at the corners. "I hope you all slept well. The children are still asleep, bless their hearts."

Chloe moved to assist with breakfast, quickly falling into a rhythm with her mother-in-law. Over the past few weeks, their relationship had flourished, strengthening a bond that transcended mere family ties. Victoria's steadfast support and gentle wisdom had become a source of strength for Chloe during this challenging time.

As they worked side by side, Victoria engaged Chloe in conversation. "You know, Chloe, I've always believed that God works in mysterious ways. When that terrible fire happened, I couldn't understand why He would allow such a thing. But seeing how it's brought us all closer together... well, I can't help but see His hand in it all."

Chloe felt a lump rise in her throat. "I understand what you mean," she replied. "It's been so difficult, losing everything. But the way everyone has united and the love we've received... it's truly a testament to God's grace."

Their conversation was interrupted by the pitter-patter of little feet. Chelsea toddled into the kitchen, her red curls a wild mess atop her head. "Mama!" she exclaimed, reaching for Chloe. Chloe scooped up her daughter and planted a kiss on her cheek. Cyrus then entered the kitchen, followed by Cullen and Carmel. The family gathered around the table and joined hands in prayer before starting their meal.

"Lord," Cyrus prayed, "we thank You for this food, for the roof over our heads, and for the love that surrounds us. We ask for Your continued guidance as we rebuild our lives. In Jesus' name, Amen."

The days spent in the Thorntons' mansion fell into a much-appreciated pattern over time, each bringing its own challenges and blessings. Chloe found herself growing closer to Victoria, their shared faith providing a strong foundation for their deepening relationship. They often sat together in the evenings, reading Bible verses that spoke of hope and renewal.

One such evening, as they sat on the porch swing, Victoria turned to Chloe with tears in her eyes. "You know," she began, her voice quivering slightly, "I always prayed for a daughter. And now, in you, God has answered that prayer in the most unexpected way."

Chloe leaned over to hug the older woman. "Oh, Victoria. You've been such a blessing to me—to us. I don't know how we would have gotten through this without you and Mr. Thornton."

Their tender moment was interrupted by Cyrus, who came out onto the porch with a worried expression. "Mom," he said, his voice laden with concern, "Dad's not feeling well. He's complaining of chest pains."

The hours that followed passed in a blur of ambulance sirens and hospital corridors. Mr. Thornton had suffered a mild heart attack, and while the prognosis was good, he would need to remain in the hospital for observation and treatment.

While sitting in the waiting room, Chloe watched Cyrus pace back and forth, worry etched on his face. She reached for his hand, pulling him down to sit beside her. "Cyrus, remember what Pastor Merchant always says: 'When we can't trace God's hand, we must trust His heart.' Your father is in God's care now."

"You're right. It's just... it's all so much, Chloe. The fire. The house-hopping. And now this..." he said with a loud sigh.

"I know, my love," Chloe soothed, resting her head on his shoulder. "But you and your mother are not alone in this. Your family is here for you, and we have each other, our faith, and a community of believers who care for us."

Challenging days become their new norm. Cyrus spent most of his time at the hospital, torn between his worry for his father and his desire to be with his family. Chloe stepped up, managing the household and caring for the children while also providing emotional support to Victoria, who was struggling with her husband's hospitalization.

One particularly trying day, Chloe found herself feeling overwhelmed. The children were fussy, the insurance paperwork for their rebuilding efforts seemed never-ending, and she missed her husband terribly. In a quiet moment, she retreated to the guest bedroom, sinking to her knees beside the bed to pray. *"Lord, I know You have a plan. I know You're working on our behalf during this storm. But Father, I'm tired. I'm scared. Please give me the strength to be what my family needs right now. Help me to be a reflection of Your love and grace. In Your Name, I pray. Amen."* When she finished praying, a peace that transcended all understanding washed over her. She felt rejuvenated, ready to face the next challenge.

As she rose from her knees, she noticed a framed Bible verse on the nightstand that she hadn't seen before:

"'For I know the plans I have for you,' declares the LORD, 'plans to prosper you and not to harm you, plans to give you hope and a future.'" ~ Jeremiah 29:11

"Confirmation, Lord. I thank You," she said humbly, placing her hand over her heart.

With renewed determination, Chloe dedicated herself fully to supporting her family. She organized a rotation of church members to provide meals and assist with the children, allowing her to spend more time at the hospital with Cyrus and his parents. She also coordinated with their insurance company and contractors, ensuring plans for their new home stayed on track. Through it all, she relied heavily on her faith, drawing strength from prayer and the supportive community surrounding her.

The days flew by, and things started to improve. Mr. Thornton's health stabilized, allowing him to return home. The plans for their new house were finalized, and the beginning construction date was set. Through it all, Chloe and Cyrus's love for each other and their faith in God remained unshaken.

One evening, as they sat together on the porch swing, Cyrus turned to Chloe, his eyes filled with love and admiration. "Chloe, I don't know if I've told you this enough, but you've been incredible through all of this. Your strength, your faith... you've been our rock."

Chloe smiled. "It hasn't been me, Cyrus; it's been God working through me. Through all of us, as a matter of fact. We've been each other's strength."

"You're right, as always," he chuckled. "You know, when I look back on this time, I think I'll remember it not for the hardships but for the love. The way our family united, the support from our church community, the deepening of our faith... it's all been so beautiful in its own way."

They fell into a comfortable silence, each with joyful thoughts drifting through the deepest recesses of their mind.

"I believe this whole experience has taught me something important," Chloe reflected, her voice gentle in the twilight. "Home isn't just a location; it's wherever we are together and surrounded by love and faith."

"Yes, yes. As long as we have that, we'll always be home," Cyrus said, pulling her closer.

In the evening's tranquility, with the soft sounds of their children's chatter and laughter wafting from inside the house, they felt truly blessed. They had lost much but had gained even more. Their love story stood as a testament to the enduring power of faith, family, and unconditional love.

Chapter Twenty: Love's Enduring Light

Virtually simultaneously with her awakening from a deep sleep, Chloe reached out, expecting to feel Cyrus' warmth beside her, only to find cool sheets. With a sigh, she sat up, her eyes landing on the empty space where her husband should have been.

It had been three weeks since Mrs. Victoria Thornton's sudden passing from a brain aneurysm, and the weight of grief still hung heavily in their home. Chloe's heart ached for Cyrus, who had been struggling to come to terms with the loss of his mother. She closed her eyes, offering a silent prayer:

'Lord, please give Cyrus strength for today. Help me to be the support he needs. Guide us through this valley of shadow and death. Amen.'

She heard the gentle creak of the floorboards outside their room. As if in response to her prayer, Cyrus appeared in the doorway, his eyes red-rimmed and tired. Without a word, Chloe opened her arms, and he crossed the room to sink into her embrace.

"I couldn't sleep," he said wearily. "I kept thinking about Mom, about all the things I wished I'd said..."

Chloe gently stroked his back. "Your mother knew how much you loved her, Cyrus. She saw it in everything you did."

They sat in silence, finding comfort in one another. Finally, Cyrus pulled back and met Chloe's gaze. "We have the grief therapy session today," he said, his voice wavering. "I... I'm not sure I'm... ready," he sobbed.

Chloe took his hand in hers, her eyes brimming with love and compassion. "We'll face this together, just like we have with everything else. Remember what Pastor Merchant says? 'God's strength is made perfect in our weakness.' We don't have to be strong on our own."

As they prepared for the day ahead, Chloe couldn't help but marvel at the journey they had been on lately: the fire that destroyed their home, Mr. Thornton's heart attack, and now, Mrs. Thornton's sudden passing. Each trial had tested their faith, resolve, and love. Yet here they were, still standing, still loving, and still believing.

The grief therapy session took place in a small, warmly lit room at their local community center. As Chloe and Cyrus settled into the circle of chairs, they noticed a young couple across from them, their hands tightly clasped together, eyes reddened from recent tears.

The therapist, Dr. Marilyn Porter, a kind-faced woman with a strikingly beautiful smile, began the session with a gentle introduction. "Today," she said, her voice calm and reassuring, "I'd like us to focus on finding hope amidst our grief. Would anyone like to share their experience?"

There was a pin-drop-quiet moment before Cyrus cleared his throat and stood. "Hello, everyone. My name is Cyrus Thornton. I... I lost my mother recently," he began, his voice quivering slightly. "It's been hard. Harder than I ever could have imagined. But..." he glanced at Chloe, drawing strength from her presence, "I'm learning that grief doesn't erase hope. My wife, my faith, and my family... they remind me that there's still light, even in the darkest moments."

As Cyrus spoke, Chloe noticed the young couple leaning forward, their eyes intensely fixed on her husband. When he finished, the woman spoke up, her voice barely above a whisper. "How? How do you do it? How do you find that hope?"

Chloe felt a nudge from the Holy Spirit, prompting her to speak. "For us, it's our faith that anchors us. We believe in a God who loves us and walks with us up every mountain and down through every valley. While He doesn't eliminate the pain, He gives us the strength to keep going."

The young man, who introduced himself as Carl, shook his head. "I used to believe in God," he said, his voice filled with bitterness, "but after losing our child, I just can't anymore. How could a loving God allow such suffering?"

Cyrus, now seated, leaned forward, his eyes filled with compassion. "I understand that feeling. I've wrestled with that same question, but I've come to realize that God doesn't cause our pain. He weeps with us and offers comfort... if we're willing to accept it."

As the session continued, Chloe and Cyrus shared more about their faith, struggles, and the hope they had found amidst their trials. They spoke of the fire that had destroyed their home, the community that had rallied around them, and the unexpected blessings they had discovered along the way. "It's not about having all the answers," Chloe explained. "It's about trusting that there is a bigger picture, even when we can't see it. It's about holding onto hope, even when everything seems hopeless."

When the session ended, Carl and his wife, Yvonne, approached Chloe and Cyrus. "Could you share more about the God you mentioned?" Yvonne asked hesitantly. "We've tried everything else, but nothing seems to help. Maybe... maybe it's time to give faith another chance."

In the following weeks, Chloe and Cyrus not only processed their own grief but also became a source of support and inspiration for others in the group. They started meeting with Carl and Yvonne outside of therapy, sharing meals, studying Scriptures together, and offering a listening ear whenever needed. One evening, as they gathered around the dinner table with Carl and Yvonne, Cyrus shared a passage from the Old Testament Book of Psalms:

"The Lord is close to the brokenhearted and saves those who are crushed in spirit." ~ Psalm 34:18.

Yvonne's eyes glistened with tears as she reached for Carl's hand. "I think I'm starting to understand what you mean about hope," she said softly. "It doesn't take away the pain but gives us a reason to keep going."

Despite their own pain and grief, Chloe felt grateful for how God used their experiences to illuminate others' darkness. It served as a powerful reminder of His ability to create beauty from ashes.

The weeks turned into months, and gradually, life began to find a new rhythm. Mr. Thornton, still mourning the loss of his wife but uplifted by his family's support, decided to move to an apartment closer to his younger sister.

"This house..." he said one evening, near tears, "it carries too many memories. It's time for it to be filled with new life and new love. I want you and Cyrus to have it, Chloe. Make it a home for your family, just like Victoria and I did for Cyrus. Maybe you can lease out your rebuilt home. I would truly appreciate it if you chose to stay here."

The transition of ownership felt bittersweet. As they helped Cyrus' father pack his belongings, each item seemed to tell a story—a piece of the life he had shared with his wife. Yet, there was also a sense of new beginnings, honoring Victoria's memory by filling the house with love and laughter once again. On the night Mr. Thornton moved out, Chloe and Cyrus stood in the empty living room, their arms around each other. The house felt different now. It was no longer just a temporary shelter; it was truly their home.

"It's strange," Cyrus mused, his voice echoing in the empty room. "I keep expecting Mom to come around the corner or hear Dad laughing from the kitchen. But at the same time, I can envision our future here. I can picture our children growing up in these rooms, creating their own memories."

"Your mom would have loved that. She always said this house was meant to be filled with family and love."

"You know," Cyrus said, turning to face her, "I've been reflecting a lot on something Pastor Merchant mentioned in his sermon last week, about how our tests can become our testimonies."

Chloe nodded, understanding dawning in her eyes. "I've thought about that, too," she admitted. "Look at how God has used our struggles to reach others, to offer hope to people like Carl and Yvonne. It's like that verse from Romans 8:28: 'And we know that in all things, God works for the good of those who love Him.'"

"I never would have imagined that losing Mom would lead us to help others find faith and build a relationship with God. It doesn't make the loss any easier but somehow gives it meaning," he replied.

As night fell, the couple went outside and settled onto the old swing that had been a fixture on the Thornton property for decades. The stars twinkled overhead, reminding them of the vastness of God's creation and the smallness of their own troubles in the grand scheme of things.

"What do you think the future holds for us, Chloe?"

"I don't know exactly, but I do know this: We'll be ready for whatever may come."

While they sat there, gently rocking and wrapped in each other's arms, Chloe felt a sense of anticipation for the days ahead. Yes, more trials and tribulations would come. Yes, there would be more moments of doubt and fear. But there would also be joy, love, and the unshakeable certainty that they were precisely where God wanted them to be.

As they drifted off to sleep that night in the home filled with cherished memories and the promise of many more, Chloe's last conscious thought was a prayer of gratitude. She prayed for strength, for the hope that continued to burn brightly in their hearts, and for light during the darkest days ahead.

Chapter Twenty-One: A Renewed Love

The gentle creaking of the porch swing filled the air as Chloe and Cyrus sat side by side, their fingers intertwined. The setting sun painted the sky in striking shades of orange, pink, and lavender hues, casting a warm glow on their faces. It had been five years since Victoria's passing, and the couple found themselves reflecting on the journey that had led them to this moment.

"I can hardly believe how much has changed since my mother passed away. How can it feel like yesterday and a lifetime ago all at once?" Cyrus asked, not expecting an answer.

"I know what you mean. Grief was so raw back then, but look at how God has worked in our lives since. We've grown so much, both as individuals and as a family," Chloe replied thoughtfully.

Their conversation turned to their children. Cullen, now a teenager, was beginning to explore his own faith with a passion that both surprised and delighted his parents. Carmel, on the brink of adolescence, was asking profound questions about God and His plan for her life. Even little Chelsea, no longer so little, was developing a sweet, simple faith that often left her parents in awe.

"Remember how worried we used to be about how the children would cope with losing their grandmother?" Cyrus mused. "I see Mom's spirit in them sometimes. Her kindness... her faith. It's like she's still with us in a way."

Chloe smiled as memories of Victoria flooded her mind. "She would have loved to see how they've grown. How we've all grown, really."

"I've been thinking a lot lately about our journey together. About all we've been through and how our love has only deepened through it all."

"What's on your mind, love?" Chloe asked with curiosity.

Cyrus took her hands in his. "I think I'd like us to renew our vows. Not with a big, fancy ceremony, but something small and intimate—a way to reaffirm our commitment to each other and to God."

Chloe nodded enthusiastically, tears streaming down her face. "Oh, Cyrus! Yes! That's a fantastic idea! It's a chance to celebrate our love and how God has remained faithful to us through everything!"

As they planned their vow renewal, their excitement grew. They chose a simple ceremony in the home's garden, with just their children, close family, and a few dear friends from the church in attendance. They would invite Pastor Merchant to officiate and write their own vows, reflecting on the journey they had taken together.

"You know," Chloe said one evening as they finalized the details, "I can't stop thinking about how different our perspectives are now compared to when we first got married. We were so young back then, so filled with hopes and dreams."

"And now, we still have hopes and dreams, but they're tempered by experience," Cyrus agreed. "We've faced loss, grief, financial struggles, and health challenges... but we've also witnessed God's faithfulness in ways we never could have imagined or even deserved."

"Exactly! This vow renewal is not just about recommitting to each other. It's also about recommitting to keeping God at the head of our marriage, home, and lives."

The day of the vow renewal arrived, bathed in warm sunshine. Their backyard was adorned with simple decorations: fairy lights strung between trees, wildflowers in mason jars, and a small flower arch where they would stand to exchange their vows.

As Chloe walked toward Cyrus, their three children beside her, she felt overwhelmed with love. Cyrus stood under the arch, waiting for his bride, his eyes brimming with tears and a wide smile that seemed to illuminate the entire yard.

Pastor Merchant began the ceremony with a prayer, thanking God for His faithfulness to Chloe and Cyrus throughout their years together. Then, it was time for them to exchange their vows.

Cyrus went first, his voice steady despite the emotion visible in his eyes. "Chloe, when we first stood before God and our loved ones to make our vows all those years ago, we had no idea what lay ahead. We've faced challenges I could never have imagined, but through it all, your love has been my anchor. You've been my partner, best friend, comfort in times of sorrow, and greatest joy in moments of happiness. Today, I recommit myself to you, promising to love you with the selfless love of Christ, to support you in all your endeavors, and to continually work to keep God at the head of our marriage. I love you more today than I did on our wedding day, and I know my love will only continue to grow."

Tears streamed down Chloe's face as she began her vows with a trembling voice. "Cyrus, our journey together has been one of growth, overcoming challenges, and a love that deepens with time. You've been my rock and safe haven in every storm we've faced. Your faith inspires me, your kindness humbles me, and your love elevates me every single day. I stand here today to reaffirm my commitment to you and our family and to keep God as the foundation of our lives. I promise to continue growing with you, to face whatever life brings us, and to love you with all that I am for all our days."

When they exchanged rings once more, symbolizing the renewal of their commitment, there wasn't a dry eye at the gathering. Their children watched with joy and reverence, witnessing the depths of their parents' love and faith.

After the ceremony, as their loved ones celebrated, Chloe and Cyrus stole a moment to be alone. They stood beneath the old oak tree in their yard—the same one that had witnessed countless moments of their life together.

"I keep thinking about how the hard times have brought us closer together, Chloe. Losing Mom was one of the most difficult things we've faced, but it also showed me the depth of your strength and love for me."

Chloe quoted verses from Romans 5:3-4: *"'We also glory in our sufferings, because we know that suffering produces perseverance; perseverance, character; and character, hope.'"* She looked at Cyrus lovingly. "Our trials have deepened our faith and love in ways that go beyond understanding."

After the guests departed, Chloe and Cyrus gathered their children for a family prayer led by Cyrus:

"Heavenly Father, we come before You with hearts full of gratitude. Thank You for Your faithfulness throughout our journey. We ask for Your continued blessings on our marriage and family. Guide us as we seek to honor You in all that we do. May our love for one another and for You continue to grow stronger with each passing day. In Jesus' Name, Amen."

The next morning, as the first light of dawn painted the sky, the family set off for the beach. It had become a tradition for them—a way to start anew after significant moments in their lives. As they strolled along the shore, the cool sand beneath their feet and the rhythmic sound of waves flowing in their ears, Chloe and Cyrus watched their children run ahead. Their joyful laughter drifted back to them in the sea's breeze.

"My love, are you ready for whatever the future holds for us?" Chloe asked, her warm hand in Cyrus'.

He smiled, keeping a watchful eye on their children. "I'm ready. With God by our side, we'll weather whatever storm is on the horizon."

The sun climbed higher in the sky, its warmth a gentle caress against their skin. Ahead, their children called for them to join in their game. With shared smiles, their parents ran to meet them. In that moment, with the endless horizon before them and the laughter of their family surrounding them, they felt the truth of what they had always known: their love, rooted in faith and tested by the fire of trials, would continue to grow and flourish—a testament to God's enduring grace in their lives.

Although their journey hadn't always been easy, it had brought them to a place filled with deep love, unwavering faith, and joyful anticipation for the days ahead.

Epilogue: A Testament to Faith and Forever Love

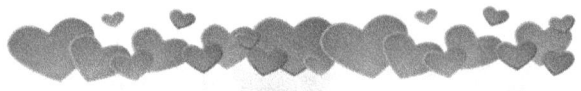

The golden rays of the setting sun painted the sky in hues of amber and rose as Chloe and Cyrus sat hand in hand on their porch swing, the gentle creaking a familiar melody to their ears. The years had etched fine lines around their eyes and sprinkled silver through their hair, yet the love reflected in their gazes remained as vibrant as ever. Before them, their four grandchildren—two girls and two boys—played in the yard, their laughter a sweet symphony echoing through the air.

"Can you believe it's been 40 years?" Cyrus mused, his voice filled with wonder. "Sometimes, it feels like just yesterday that we were beginning our journey together."

Chloe squeezed his hand, a sweet smile playing on her lips. "And what a journey it's been, my love. Through it all, God has been faithful."

Sitting in comfortable silence, their minds wandered back over the tapestry of their lives together. They remembered the early days of their marriage, filled with hopes and dreams for the future. They recalled the devastating fire that had destroyed their first home. They reminisced about the loss of Mrs. Victoria Thornton—a wound that had healed but left a tender scar, reminding them of the preciousness of life and the importance of cherishing every moment.

"You know," Cyrus said thoughtfully, "I've been thinking a lot about that verse from 1 Corinthians lately. The one about faith, hope, and love."

Chloe nodded, the familiar words flowing effortlessly from her lips. "'And now these three remain: faith, hope, and love. But the greatest of these is love.' It has always been one of my favorites."

"I believe I understand it much better now than ever," Cyrus continued. "Our faith has been our foundation, providing us strength when we felt weak and guidance when we felt lost. Hope has been our beacon, illuminating even our darkest moments. But love... love has been the thread that's woven it all together."

Reflecting on their journey, both marveled at how their faith had grown and deepened over the years. They remembered countless moments when they turned to prayer in times of joy and sorrow, finding comfort and guidance in God's presence. They recalled the many Sunday mornings spent in church, their children by their sides, soaking in the wisdom of Scripture and the fellowship of their community.

"Do you remember how worried we were when Cullen started questioning his faith during his high school years? We were so afraid he would turn away from God entirely," Chloe said, her eyes twinkling with the memory.

Cyrus chuckled, shaking his head. "And now, look at him—a pastor leading others to Christ, a husband, and a devoted father of two boys. God certainly works in mysterious ways!"

Their conversation shifted to their other two children. Carmel, who had inherited her mother's compassionate heart, was a social worker assisting families in crisis and a married mother of beautiful twin girls. Chelsea, the artist, painted nature's beauty as a testament to the wonder of God's creation, traveling and selling her artistic creations to galleries around the globe.

"We've been blessed beyond measure," Chloe said, her gratitude shining through every word. "Not just with our children and grandchildren, but with the life we've built. It hasn't always been easy, but I wouldn't change a single second of it."

Cyrus stood, offering his hand to his wife. "Come, my love. Let's take a walk."

Hand in hand, they walked down the familiar path leading to the beach, their grandchildren racing ahead, filled with excitement for the adventure. The sound of waves lapping at the shore welcomed them, a soothing rhythm that spoke of consistency amidst change.

As they walked along the water's edge, their feet leaving temporary imprints in the sand, Chloe and Cyrus found themselves marveling at how God had worked in their lives. They saw His hand in the significant moments—the births of their children, their milestones, and their accomplishments. However, they also recognized His presence in the small, everyday occurrences: a kind word from a stranger, a moment of unexpected beauty in the garden, and the comfort of a loved one's embrace.

"I believe one of the greatest blessings of our journey has been how our trials have shaped and deepened our faith. Each challenge we've encountered has brought us closer to God and to each other," Chloe said, her voice nearly lost in the sound of the waves.

With understanding shining in his eyes, Cyrus quoted Romans 5:3-4: "'We also glory in our sufferings, because we know that suffering produces perseverance; perseverance, character; and character, hope.' Sweetheart, our trials have shaped us, refined us, and made us who we are today. God's Word never lies."

As they watched their grandchildren playing at the water's edge, squealing with delight as the cool waves lapped at their feet, Chloe and Cyrus felt a deep sense of gratitude. They had weathered countless storms together, faced loss and heartache, and celebrated joys, both big and small. Through it all, faith had been their foundation, and their love for each other reflected God's love for them.

"I wonder what advice we would give our younger selves if we could go back in time," Cyrus mused, his eyes focused on the horizon where the sea met the sky.

Chloe remained silent for a few moments. "I think I would encourage them to trust in God's plan, even when it doesn't seem clear. I would also advise them to rely on one another and their faith during difficult times and to never take a moment for granted."

The sky darkened, and the stars began to twinkle overhead. Chloe and Cyrus gathered their grandchildren and made their way back to the Thornton family mansion. The path was familiar, yet each step seemed like a continuation of the journey they had begun so many years ago.

Back on their porch, with the little ones tucked safely in bed, Chloe and Cyrus found themselves once again hand in hand, gazing at the star-studded sky. The vastness of the universe above them reminded them of the greatness of God's love—a boundless love that guided them through every step of their lives.

Afterword

C hloe and Cyrus' story draws to a close, and we are left with a powerful reminder of the enduring nature of faith, hope, and love. Their journey inspires and encourages us to reflect on our own lives and how God has been faithful to us.

Perhaps you, dear reader, can reflect on your own journey. How have you witnessed God's hand moving in your life? In what ways have your trials strengthened your faith and deepened your relationships? Like Chloe and Cyrus, you have a unique story of God's faithfulness—a testament to His enduring love and grace.

Having reached the conclusion of this story, take a moment to reflect on the following thought-provoking questions:

- ❖ How has faith in God influenced your journey through life's joys and challenges?
- ❖ How can your experiences, including both triumphs and trials, serve as a testament to God's love and faithfulness for others?

Remember: Your story is still unfolding. Every day presents a new chance to trust in God's perfect plan, to rely on your faith, and to love wholeheartedly. May you, like Chloe and Cyrus, discover strength in your challenges, joy in your blessings, and a continually deepening faith that guides you through all of life's teachings.

As you close this book and turn the pages of your own life, may you be inspired to live a life that is a testament to faith, hope, and love, for in the end, these three remain—and the greatest of these is...

"My beloved friends, let us continue to love each other since love comes from God. Everyone who loves is born of God and experiences a relationship with God. The person who refuses to love doesn't know the first thing about God, because God is love—so you can't know Him if you don't love."

1 John 4:7-8
The Message Bible Translation

www.ingramcontent.com/pod-product-compliance
Lightning Source LLC
Chambersburg PA
CBHW060421260626
47161CB00005B/1723